THREE PUMPS

AND A

PLACE TO STAY

Myles Allpress

ISBN 978-0-6156-0506-7

Printed in the United States of America.
First edition, March 2012.

3 5 7 9 10 8 6 4 2

Contents

To Dan, this is for you, my friend.

To Laura, Flash, Kimmy, Johnny, and Rodrigo,
without you this story would not have been possible.

To my Mamma, my darling Sarah, and Simon,
thank you for all your advice, help and editing.

To Linda, thank you for correcting my English.

To Dad, Charlotte, Marcus, Sophia, and Lillian
thank you for all your love and support.

I love you all.

Dan, Kimmy and Thailand

I awoke on one exceptionally hot Saturday morning with a terrible hangover. My mouth was dry and tasted like a cat had defecated in it sometime during the night. When I tried to open my eyes, they stung from the sun shining through my too-thin curtains for the state I was in. I stumbled into the lounge to find Dan fast asleep on my couch, dribbling saliva over the leather, but I didn't care; I was too hungover to care. I picked up his jeans off the floor and searched his pockets. Finding a half-empty, crumpled packet of Marlboro Lights, I walked outside onto the balcony to light one up. As the smoke filled my lungs, I tried to remember the previous night—the night that had done this to me.

I'd finished work and met Dan for a beer at the Irish pub in the Mercantile Hotel, across the road from where I work. It was a beautiful summer night, and, as always, one beer turned into two, two into three, and so on. I didn't have a girlfriend or wife, so I had no one to answer to. No one to slow me down, to incessantly call me with things I'd heard coming from the mobile phones of my work peers as I watched them disappear one by one out the door. Things like "I think you've had enough now, honey, come home, please," or "Get your ass home now, or you're on the fucking couch." Dan didn't either, so I could understand why he was perplexed that I wanted to head home so early.

"I wouldn't mind heading back to Bondi, dude," I said, glancing at my watch.

"What? We're just getting started, fuck-knuckle," he said, staring at me like I'd just pissed on his leg. I couldn't help but crack a smile. He was a funny bastard, and I never stopped laughing around him.

We had met a couple of years ago, when he started working at the same ad agency as I in Sydney. Dan had since moved on to another job, but we remained the best of friends.

"I'm not going home, you prick. There *are* pubs there, you know."

"Yeah, and you'll drink one beer and piss off to bed."

"When the fuck have I ever done that?"

"I can't remember off the top of my head . . . I'm just preempting."

"I won't. I promise." I grinned at him.

"For fuck's sake, Myles. Something good—no, something great better happen."

"Dan, me ol' mucker, being with me *is* something great." I wrapped my arm around him. He hated it when I hugged him—or so he said.

"It's definitely something," he mumbled, before shrugging my arm off his shoulder and gulping the rest of his beer.

We caught a cab to Bondi Beach that I stopped down the road from the Beach Road Hotel—the meter read 20 even, and we could walk the rest of the way. Dan and I scurried along in silence, dodging people wandering the streets in various states of inebriation. With only a few meters between us and our next beer, a guy with a thick Irish accent stopped us in our tracks. He said, "Hey . . . you guys drink in the Mercantile, right?"

We turned to face a tall, young bloke with a can of beer in his hand. "How'd you know that?" I replied.

"I work there."

"Of course you do. You're Irish," said Dan, trying to take the piss, but sounding borderline racist.

"Yeah, it helps," he laughed, fortunately, seeing the funny side of Dan's warped sense of humor. "I thought so, I see you in there quite a bit."

"Oh, yeah, I remember you, dude," I said, trying my best to sound sincere, but, in all honesty, I couldn't—for the life of me—remember him.

"What are you guys up to?"

"Well, as it happens, we just got back from the Merc and now we're heading to the Beachy for a few more."

An awkward silence grew as our friend just stood, nodding and smiling. Feeling obliged and almost pressured to do so, I asked, "You wanna come?"

"Oh, thanks, but I'm heading back to my gaff." He pointed in the opposite direction of the pub. "There are a few of me boys back there, you know . . . drinking and playing guitar."

"Oh, okay . . . no worries." Feeling oddly rejected, I tried to garner some sort of support from Dan with my eyes, but he was preoccupied with lighting a cigarette in the stiff breeze.

I don't know if our new friend noticed or if he just felt obligated as I had only moments before, but he sheepishly asked, "Um, why don't you guys come with? You're more than welcome."

"Oh, yeah? I quickly glanced at my watch; it read 11:30 p.m. I made a quick calculation in my head on how many beers we could get in before the pub closed at one, maybe three or four if we were lucky. Then again, they start ushering everyone out around twelve, so maybe only two.

"What do you reckon, Dan?" I asked, turning to my mate as he continued to fruitlessly light his cigarette. Our new friend and I watched for what seemed like an age, as he turned around and around trying to block the wind with his back. Finally, the lighter sparked to life long enough for him to light up. "Dan?" I impatiently said again.

"Fuck it, why not?" he finally replied, after taking a drag. "I hate that pub anyway."

"Yeah, come on," said our new friend, walking away and gesturing at us to follow. "I'm Patrick, by the way."

"Of course you . . . " started Dan, before I quickly interrupted him with an elbow to his chest.

Dan mouthed the word, "What?" with a mischievous grin and shrugged his shoulders.

"I'm Myles, and this ginger twat is Dan," I said, glowering at Dan.

We followed Patrick, turning down Carlewis Street, and then down a driveway that happened to be directly across the road from where I lived. "Hey, you live right across the road from me," I said, pointing at my apartment.

"No shit? Weird that I've never seen you around till now, eh?"

"That's because I'm always in the Merc!" I said, laughing, like it was pure comedic genius—although it clearly wasn't, made apparent from Dan's discombobulated look.

Patrick led us into a small, cramped and rundown apartment

that can only be described as a prison cell with a fridge and a kitchen sink. There were a bunch of topless blokes sitting on an old couch that looked like it had been rescued from the rubbish dump, singing songs to a guitar and drinking cans of beer and wine from four-liter boxes. They must have been rather fond of that particular wine, because they had constructed a wall of empty wine boxes; there must been two hundred or so, neatly stacked all the way to the ceiling.

The room went dead silent at the sight of us. "All right, lads? I found these two out on the street. They're me mates from the Merc," said Patrick, before he introduced every one of them to Dan and me.

Each of the boys gave us a quick nod of acknowledgment and, satisfied that we were harmless, went back to their singing and drinking.

"The fridge is over there, lads, help yourself." Patrick pointed to an old fridge in one of the four corners of the room that was covered in postcards and photos of him and his friends, pulling stupid faces and poses while drinking in various places around the world. But, there was one postcard that really caught my eye. It was a picture of a beach with light cyan water kissing the whitest sand I'd ever seen; tall palm trees dotted the horizon and one word emblazoned through the middle: Thailand.

"Myles, are you going to hump that fridge or get me a beer?" said Dan, snapping me from my gaze.

"Calm down," I said, and lobbed him a can. "This is all right, eh? Free beer."

"Yeah, shit like this happens to me all the time." Dan cracked his can open and quickly took a sip before it overflowed. "Like the last time I was in Bondi, remember? I ended up losing you at the Bondi Hotel." Dan slowly lowered his brow, but kept a steady gaze on me. "Or maybe you fucking ditched me."

I rolled my eyes. "Go on, dickhead."

"Well, some random dude tapped me on the shoulder and asked whether I could roll joints. The next thing you know, I'm at some random apartment rolling and smoking pot with four backpackers from Sweden."

"Oh, yeah. I vaguely remember you telling me that. What happened?"

"I ended up rambling on about nothing till I had smoked all of their weed." He paused to gaze into the mouth of his beer like it was the fondest memory he had. He finally looked up at me with a grin, and said, "I bet that guy rued tapping me on the shoulder that night."

"Nothing like free drugs, eh, bro?" I laughed.

"Or beer!" Dan held out his can at me.

I agreed with a wink, and hit my can against his before taking another swig.

We continued to drink into the wee hours of the morning. Every now and again, we would nod and smile to the others as they sang, or sometimes pretended to sing along—just to disguise the fact we were just there for the beer—and we didn't stop till the fridge was empty.

I don't remember what time it was when the two of us stumbled across the road to my apartment, or fumbled with the key in the lock, or finally passed out. What I do remember was that we were drunk—blind drunk.

I flicked my cigarette over the balcony; it hadn't helped with how I was feeling at all. I squinted at the sky with my sore eyes. It was a piercing blue, and not a cloud in sight. The temperature was around 35 degrees and, coupled with my hangover, it was making me feel a little nauseous—I hate feeling that bad when the day is that good.

I wandered inside and stared at my redheaded friend slumbering on the couch. "Mate, it's a fucking beautiful day," I said, as I opened the blinds to wake him up. "We've got to get out into it."

"I think I'd rather crawl into a fucking cave, pal," he said, squinting at me, trying to shield the sun with his hand.

"Fuck that. Come on, get up, dickhead, let's go to the beach for a swim."

"I fucking hate the . . . " but Dan couldn't finish; my phone wouldn't let him. Finding it on the floor, I read Swanny's name on the display; he was a guy we both knew through work. "Swanny, what's doin?" I asked when I answered it.

"Dude, are you going to Johnny's barbecue today?" Johnny was another mutual friend who lived in Bronte, a couple of suburbs south. "I can't stay all day, so I'm going to drive. I can pick you up on the way if you want?"

"Dude, I was literally just thinking what a perfect day it is for one. Hang on, though, Dan's with me." I held the phone to my chest and kicked Dan in the ass. "Oi, are you keen for a barbie at Johnny's?"

He pulled his head out from under a pillow. "I dunno, who's going . . . any chicks?"

I rolled my eyes and sighed, "Hang on." I put the phone back to my ear. "Swanny, are there any chicks going?"

"Yeah, I'm picking up a couple on the way."

"He's picking some up on the way, Don Juan DeMarco, do you want to go or not? I'm going."

"Yeah, yeah, whatever," he said, finally sitting upright and rubbing his ginger hair.

"Swanny, we're on. Come and grab us."

I hung up the phone and grinned at my friend on the couch who just stared back at me like he was the recipient of an overnight lobotomy. "Get in the shower, and hurry the fuck up," I said.

"Okay, okay. Settle down."

Twenty minutes, later we heard Swanny's car honk in the street and clambered out to meet him. "Hot enough, for you, lads?" he asked, as we piled into his car.

"My sweat is sweating," said Dan.

"What the fuck does that even mean?"

"Well, my sweat has bacteria in it, and that bacteria is sitting in my sweat sweating. In fact, there is probably bacteria in my sweat's bacteria that's sweating, too."

"Jesus, Dan, where the fuck do you even come up with that shit?"

Bondi Beach was teeming with people as we drove to the southernmost end, as is always the case when it's hot. "I hate Bondi when it gets this busy," I said quietly, as I leaned my chin on my elbow out of the rear window, trying in vain to get a breeze going on my face. "I'm rather glad to get out of it for the day."

"What are you crying about back there?" said Dan.

"I said, I'm happy to be getting out of Bondi for the day. It's too busy."

"Jesus, Myles, you couldn't wait to get down here last night and now you can't wait to fucking leave."

I sighed but kept my mouth shut. Swanny double-parked outside an apartment block and honked his horn. "I'm pretty sure this is it," he said, peering at the house like he had x-ray vision and was able to scan every apartment for the girls.

We waited quietly. Then, five minutes later, two young girls emerged from the apartment block chatting to each other all the way to the car. Swanny introduced us, "Myles, Dan, this is Kimmy and Shannon."

We all greeted each other with a stock-standard, "Hey."

"Anyone need me to stop for booze?" asked Swanny, as we continued on our way.

"Yes!" we all cried in unison.

We stopped halfway up Bondi Road at a liquor store; Swanny stayed in the car while the rest of us went in to buy alcohol for the barbecue. "What do you want, brother?" I asked Dan, as we perused the beer fridge.

"A case ought to do it, don't you think?"

"Yeah, but what flavor?"

"Oh, Coopers."

"You and me, we're like telepathic or something," I said, pointing two fingers at his forehead then at mine, again and again.

"Myles, that's all we ever drink, you fucking idiot," he said, with a grin and a shake of his head.

"Calm down, sweetheart." I grabbed a case of Coopers, and two minutes later, Dan, the beers, and I were in the car ready to go. The girls, however, were nowhere to be seen. Five minutes went by, then ten. Dan grew impatient. "What the fuck are they doing in there, comparing tampons?"

Dan has a way of saying things that are both right and extremely inappropriate, and though it might sound malicious or aggressive, that's not his intention at all; it's just the way he speaks. "Who are these two anyway, Swanny?"

"Jesus, Dan, do you kiss your mother with that mouth? They're friends of mine. Kimmy, the brunette, she was dating a mate of mine who recently returned to the States. I don't really know Shannon that well, she's Kimmy's friend." Before Swanny could say anymore, they finally returned to the car with just a six-pack between them.

Dan looked over his shoulder into the backseat with a face of bewilderment, and said in his sarcastic best, "Are you right there, ladies? You didn't get lost or anything, did you? Would you like a hand with that?"

"No, thanks," they said together, letting his sarcasm fly harmlessly over their heads.

I was in the back seat with the girls and, as we continued on, I tried my best to converse with them. "So, where are you gals from then?"

"New York," replied Kimmy.

As soon as she told me that, it immediately reminded me of a story that my little sister's boyfriend, Flash once told me. He said, "You know . . . a funny thing about Americans is, that whenever you ask them where they're from, when they're out-side of the States, they never say the United States, or America for that matter. They'll always just tell you what state they're from and, for some reason, I find that incredibly irritating."

Flash and my little sister, Laura, have travelled the world extensively, and had subjected me to their many stories over dinners and beers.

Flash elaborated, "We were in Spain once, chatting to a guy who was from Indiana, as he put it. But I thought, fuck it, and asked him where Indiana was? He simply replied, 'The Midwest.' So I, of course, asked him where the Midwest was. He replied, 'The States, the United States of America. You know, that huge country in between Canada and Mexico,' re-ally slowly, like I was stupid. I calmly said that I knew where Canada was as I'd been there before, and that the next time I was there, I'd have to pop down to check out the United States. He stopped talking to me after that."

"New York, huh? Cool." I immediately looked away and

rolled my eyes—truly disappointed with myself. I wasn't as quick as Flash, not with a hangover anyway. "So, what are you doing in Australia?"

"I'm here on a working holiday as a fashion designer. But, I'm doing more holiday than working."

"I think I like you Kimmy," said Dan, leaning over the back of his seat with a stupid grin on his face. This time my eyes rolled at him, and I kept my mouth shut for the rest of the journey.

Johnny was standing in his driveway ready to greet us when we pulled up. We shook hands and 'man-hugged,' which consists of your right hands grasping each other's thumbs, and then pressed between your chests, thus creating enough space between your bodies to ensure your genitals don't touch. Meanwhile, your other hand firmly taps his back around three or four times in firm and quick succession. Johnny then showed us to a barbecue area out the back of his apartment block; it was a little concrete area equipped with a table, chairs and, of course, a barbecue. The booze was put on ice, and I immediately started to work on relieving my hangover.

As the day wore on, more guests started to arrive, and my hangover quickly subsided, leaving me feeling convivial and much like the night before—drunk. At one point, I placed an arm around Dan, and asked with a grin, "Hey, brother, how's it going?"

"Not bad . . . I'm pretty drunk again." He said apathetically, more concerned with trying to get my arm off his shoulder.

"It's been a cracker of a summer, hasn't it?"

"I suppose." He gave me a suspicious look. "Why? Where's this going?"

"I reckon we should go on a trip somewhere together. You know . . . a holiday."

"You're not turning gay for me, are you?"

"Dan, even if you and I were the last men on earth, I wouldn't turn gay for you. In fact, I'd rather die by masturbation than turn gay for you. No, I just don't want the summer to end along with the fun we're having. Come winter, we should piss off somewhere."

"Where?"

"I don't know—somewhere hot and cheap like Thailand."

"Thailand?"

"Yeah, I can't get this fucking beach I saw on that Irish guy's fridge out of my head. Besides, I've always wanted to go to Thailand. Apparently you can buy beer there for a dollar."

"A dollar, huh?" Dan suddenly perked up. "Fuck it, why not? Come to think of it, my old man's got a shit-ton of frequent-flier points that are about to expire. He offered them to me the other day, so we could probably fly for free."

"That's what I'm talking about!" I offered Dan a fist bump, much to his disgust; like hugs, he hates that sort of thing. But, he awkwardly obliged and punched my knuckles.

"Hey, are you going to Thailand?" interrupted Kimmy, during our fist bump. Unbeknownst to us, she had overheard our whole conversation.

"Thinking about it," I replied.

"Cool. Um, can I tag along? I've been really wanting to go for like ever, but no one will go with me."

"Kimmy, if you want to come to Thailand with us, you can fucking well come to Thailand with us," said Dan, surprisingly stern and, at the same time, punched his fist into his hand.

Startled, I cocked my eyebrow and said, "Settle down, son, we're not storming the Reichstag."

"When were you guys thinking of going?"

"Don't know . . . winter sometime probably. Like, April or

May?" I said.

"May would be perfect," she said, smiling and clapping her hands, "my visa expires in June, so I have to go home to New York."

"Where's New York?"

"Huh?"

"Never mind. What's your number? We'll stay in touch, then."

"Nice work, pal," whispered Dan, elbowing me in the ribs after Kimmy and I swapped numbers.

"Mate, there's no way a young chick like that is going to travel *all* the way to Thailand with a couple of guys she's only just met."

"Yeah? Well, at least you got her number—she's hot."

Laura and Flash

ess than a month after Johnny's barbecue, I moved in with my little sister, Laura, and her boyfriend, Flash. It was just around the corner from my old place in Bondi Beach. My lease was up, and I was bored with living on my own anyway.

My little sister had moved to Sydney from New Zealand around 2001 with our older sister, Charlotte. I missed them both terribly, so I followed them across the ditch a couple of years later.

Laura has a wonderful, no-bullshit personality and doesn't stand for any nonsense. If there's something she doesn't approve of, she'll let you know. She's very assertive, very stubborn, but happens to be always right and would subsequently keep Flash and me in check.

Every night when I arrived home, Flash would characteristically welcome me in, which actually became the best part of my whole day. As soon as I opened the door, he'd yell at the top of his voice, "Hello? Hello?"

I'd reply, "Hello?"

"Mylesie, is that you? Mylesie? Mylesieeeee. Welcome home, brother, it's so good to see you." He would then embrace me as I walked into the room. Laura would giggle and shake her head, but he would do this literally every day without fail. I remember coming home late one night, rather drunk, when Flash had been drinking too—only he'd fallen asleep in a re-cliner watching television. When I walked into the lounge, he stirred awake and slurred with half-open eyes, "Hello? Myl-eshe? Mylshee? Home, brother . . . welcome." He then fell back to sleep. Like I said, every day without fail.

Flash is an Australian—unlike Laura and I, who are New Zealanders—which also makes him a sports-fanatic, who likes nothing better than to watch a heated sporting scrap between our two countries. The three of us would spend many an hour in the pub watching sport and debating. Dan would join us from time to time, but he hates sport.

"What kind of Australian are you?" asked Flash, one par-ticular night during a rugby match.

"One that hates sport."

"Why?"

"I don't know. I was never really good at it."

"Mate, you don't have to be good at it to watch it. In fact, you could strive to be Australia's number one sport watcher. That way, you'll finally be good at something sporty."

"Look, if you two knob-jockeys want to watch blokes run-ning around a park in skin-tight shorts fondling each other's balls, then fine, that's your prerogative. I'm quite happy drink-ing my beer over here without having to engage in homoerotic activities with you two, thank you."

"What the fuck?"

"Forget about it, Flash, I've tried before, it's no use," I interrupted.

"I want Australia to divorce him. Is that possible?"

"It's okay, Flash, let it go . . . I'll look into it."

During dinner one night, I mentioned my potential holiday plans to Laura, and Flash. "So, Dan and I are talking about heading over to Thailand for a couple of weeks. Do you guys wanna come too?"

"Fuck, yeah, of course we'll come," said Flash, without hesitation. "If anything, to protect you two from yourselves."

"Whatever do you mean?"

"Seriously? Think about it. You and Dan in Thailand?"

"Yeah, I guess you're right," I said, after taking a moment to think about the last couple of months of drunken debauchery Dan and I had shared together.

"Even so, we've been struggling with ideas for a holiday this year. Besides, it's my favorite Asian country. We've been there what, three or four times, right, babe?" said Laura.

"Yep, so when do you want to go, big fella?"

"I'm not sure, some time in winter I think . . . maybe May?"

"May, hmm." Flash rubbed his chin a bit. "It might start to rain on the east side around then, best to stay west, but May's good—not too hot."

Over the next few months, the four of us threw a few dates around, the length of time we'd stay, and where we would go once we got there. However, nothing got set in stone.

One day, in the middle of March, I received an email from Dan: "Hey, Myles, when the fuck are we going to Thailand?"

"Hey, I haven't really thought about it to be honest, mate,

I've been too busy. What about mid-May, like we said in the beginning?"

Twenty minutes later, Dan emailed me a plane ticket, which was two flights, on May 15, to Bangkok Thailand.

I immediately picked up the phone and rang him. "Jesus Christ, bro, I haven't even requested my holidays yet, what the fuck?"

"Well, you're pissing around, let's just do this already."

"How the hell did you get them? And so fast?"

"I told you. My old man has millions of frequent-flier miles that he has to use. I just emailed him the dates and he sorted it out for us."

"Fuck. Sorry, bro." I quickly calmed down at the realization that he had not only finalized our trip to Thailand, but he was flying me there for free. "You're right, I've been procrastinating."

"If I'd have left everything to you, we'd never get there, and it was your idea, for fuck's sake."

"Thanks, brother—and tell your old man he's a goddamn legend."

"I will, dude,"

That night I told Laura and Flash what had happened and that Saturday, May 15, was when we were all going to Thailand.

"You lucky bastard, a free ticket, eh?" said Flash.

"I know. I owe him big time."

"Babe, we better book ours too, then," said Laura.

"Fuck, yeah, let's do this."

And they did.

Within a week of Dan buying my ticket, a weird thing happened. I received a text, completely out of the blue. "Hey, Myles, I don't know if you remember me, Kimmy? We met at

Johnny's barbecue. I was wondering if you were still going to Thailand?"

Her timing was impeccable. "Of course I remember you, and yes, we're still going to Thailand. In fact, we booked our tickets last week. We're leaving on May 15 for two weeks."

"Cool. Is it still okay if I tag along?"

"Of course you can. My sister, Laura, and her boyfriend, Flash, are coming too."

"Wait, your sister's boyfriend's name is Flash? That's badass."

"Yeah, and they've been many times before, so you'll be safe with us."

"I'll text you when I've booked my ticket then. I'm so excited."

That weekend, I met Dan at the pub, and explained to him that Kimmy was coming too.

"No shit, just texted you out of the blue, huh?" he asked.

"Yeah, I was quite surprised. Perfect timing, eh?"

Dan slowly placed his beer on a beer coaster, carefully making sure that it was dead center. "You're going to sleep with her," he suddenly blurted. "You're going to sleep with her, and I'm going to be on holiday with two fucking couples."

"What? No, I won't."

"Yes, you will, I know you too well."

"I won't. I promise."

Dan took a sip of his beer, holding his gaze steadfastly on mine. "If you do, I'll be pissed."

"What else can I say, mate? I'm not going to sleep with her. Besides, if I recall correctly, you're the one who told her, and I quote, 'If you want to come to Thailand, fucking well come,' or did you not?"

"You know, maybe *I* could? She is pretty cute, eh?"

"Yeah, right. I assured I'd look after her, and that includes keeping her away from you."

When it came to the particulars of what we'd do or where we'd go once we got to Thailand, I left all of that to Laura and Flash. All I wanted to do was sit on a white sand beach, eat delicious food, drink dollar beers, and swim in crystal-clear water.

I wasn't going to Thailand to find myself, to be enlightened or to be that friend we all have who goes to another country for a week and comes back a different person—not physically different but annoyingly different, interrupting every conversation with, "[insert country] wasn't a holiday, it was journey of discovery." Or, "Oh, the [insert food or beverage] is so much better in [insert country]." However, by the same token, I didn't fancy myself as a tourist either. I didn't want to stay in fancy hotels and have an itinerary for every other day, like guided bus expeditions or tours of temples and other landmarks, or be that guy who walks around with a large wad of cash only to haggle over the meager price of a hand-carved wooden elephant or a fake Swiss watch.

Sure, you could argue that sitting on an island paradise surrounded by tourists and travelers is, well, a touristy thing to do. However, if I did it on a tight budget, roughed it and slept in cockroach-infested bungalows, it might give me the illusion that I was a bona fide traveler. A traveler with stories of hardship and near-death experiences in rarely visited countries around the world. The stories that I'd heard every night over dinner from Laura and Flash.

Dan, on the other hand, wanted to visit temples, markets and do the very touristy things I didn't. "Mate, when we get there, we've got to pat tigers. I've heard you can pat real tigers over there," he said, one night over a beer. Or he emailed me with, "They've got massive temples, so we've got to go to some temples for sure." Another night he rang me while I was on the bus heading home after work. "What about a full-moon party—have you heard of those? We have to go to a full-moon party."

While in the Merc one night, he said, "Markets! They have lots of markets with cheap clothes and shit. We've got to go to some markets." But I'd had enough, and I was trying to watch a game of rugby on the TV.

"Dan, shut the fuck up. I'm not the minister of fucking tourism for Thailand. Let's just bloody get there, shall we?"

"Settle down, I'm just excited."

"Fuck me. You're going to be that guy, aren't you?"

"What guy?"

"Walking around in cargo pants and a polo shirt with sweat patches under your arms and down your back, a fucking camera on a lanyard and all your shit safe and sound in a . . . "

"In a what?"

" . . . A fucking belt-bag."

"Piss off! I don't even own a camera, let alone a belt-bag."

My face softened, and I smirked. "You better not."

Laura and Flash had it all sorted anyway. "We should stay in Bangkok for one or two nights, and then catch a train or bus south to Kho Phangan. That side is best, weather-wise, this time of year. We could then travel back to Bangkok for another night or two before we fly home."

"Is that all right with you, Daniel?" I asked, after they'd explained it to the both of us.

"Are there any temples or markets where we're going?"

"Dan, it's Thailand, you can't walk five fucking meters without seeing a temple or walking into a market," explained Flash.

"Where we're staying in Bangkok *is* a big market, Dan," said Laura, placing a reassuring hand on his arm.

"Okay, but as long as I get to go to at least one temple."

Dan, you're a fucking atheist, for Christ's sake," I sighed. "Besides, we'll be too drunk to go to a fucking temple."

You Can't Swim in Ciggies

When Friday, May 14, finally arrived, I bid Laura and Flash farewell before heading to work; they were flying out that afternoon, arriving in Bangkok at 1:00 Saturday morning. They said they would organize a hotel and be waiting for Dan and me to get there. We were flying out at 7:00 a.m. on Saturday and arriving in Bangkok at 8:00 that same night. Dan's frequent-flier tickets had us stopping over in Hong Kong, which was about a four-hour detour—not ideal, but free nonetheless. Kimmy left Saturday night, arriving at 1:00 a.m. Sunday. Dan and I had agreed to pick her up from the airport to ensure she got to the hotel safe and sound, since she was all alone.

As planned, Dan and I met outside the airport terminal at around 5:00 a.m. It was still dark as we both lit cigarettes. I looked Dan over, and the first thing I noticed was his bag. I mean, mine was small, but Dan's was tiny; it was what you'd expect a five-year-old to have on his first day of school. I asked him, "Is that all you're bringing?"

"Yeah," he said, and held up his wee bag for me to get a better look at it. "Why?"

"It's fucking tiny. What's in there?"

"You know? A couple of pairs of undies, a couple of T-shirts, a pair of jeans, my toilet bag and my camcorder. The usual shit."

"For a night over at your fucking girlfriend's."

"What do you mean?"

"What about shorts or swimmers? Or even jandals, for Christ's sake? You do know we're going to a beach, don't you?"

"What the fuck are jandals?"

"Thongs, flip-flops, jandals. Let's not get into semantics."

"I don't own swimmers or *jandals*," he said, making quote marks with his fingers.

"How can you live in Sydney without owning a pair of jandals, let alone a pair of swimmers? What are you, a fucking cat?"

"I'll just buy all that shit once we get there. Do you know how cheap everything is over there? You can buy ciggies for like three dollars."

"You can't swim in ciggies, you fuckwit."

"Look, swimmers are probably two dollars, and jandals probably grow on trees."

Suddenly weary of it all, I extinguished my cigarette on a rubbish bin. "Come on, mate, let's check in."

After passing through customs without a hitch, we perused the various duty-free shops' vast selection of perfume, alcohol, cigarettes and very large Toblerone bars. Closer to our gate, we stopped for some breakfast, and it was around this time that Dan started suffering nicotine withdrawal. Dan smokes a lot. It's one of those things he loves and freely admits. He likes to think of it as a hobby, and according to him, it's the only one he's ever stuck with. Dan would go a pack-a-day easy, two if he were drinking.

"Do you know if they have smoking rooms in this airport?" he asked, nervously looking around.

"Not in Sydney, bro. They banned all that shit years ago."

I noticed a look of fear spread over his face, and his eyes glazed over as if he were staring at nothing. I knew he was slowly counting the hours in his head before he would be able to smoke again. "You'll be right, bro," I said, with a smile, snapping him from his thoughts. "I'm pretty sure they have them in Hong Kong. They love smoking over there."

Dan offered a smile back, but I knew he'd be freaking out soon. I also wondered how he'd go on the plane, because Dan is one of those people who can't sit still for too long. He's fine if he can occupy himself with a drink or smoke, or if he's conversing with someone, but if nothing happens for about five minutes, he gets anxious and starts pacing about while scratching his head. He reminds me of a Tasmanian Devil I once saw when I visited the zoo in Sydney; it was obviously stressed about being in such a small enclosure, and all it did was run around and around in the same direction until it wore a track in the grass.

We finally got to our gate, and, while we were waiting to board, Dan's mother gave him one last call before he departed Australian shores. From what I could gather, she was worried and giving him a few last minute "watch-outs."

"Mum, I'll be fine, for fuck's sake," he muttered into the phone. "No, what am I, a fucking idiot? Yes. Yes. *Yes!* No. Fuck, yes, okay bye, no, fucking bye, yes *bye.*" Dan glanced at me before whispering, "I love you, too."

When he ended the call, he grabbed the camcorder from his tiny little bag, flipped it open and started to film me. "Say something," he said.

I stared at the little red light above the lens, and a cold rush of nervousness engulfed me. What if I made a fool of myself, what if I look like shit? These thoughts, and many others, rushed through my head at a million miles a second. I started to stammer, "Well . . . um . . . I . . . I. Here are at the airport. I . . . we're going to Thailand."

Dan slowly looked up from the little view screen with his mouth open. "You're a real fucking wordsmith, aren't you, pal? Jesus Christ, I've never felt so awkward in all my life." Dan mouthed the word, "Wow," and packed the camera back into his wee bag.

"Well, I hate those fucking things. I freeze in front of them."

"You don't just freeze, mate, you become a blubbering idiot."

"You might want to leave that in your bag from now on."

"You reckon? Jesus, Myles, harden the fuck up," he said grinning.

We boarded our flight and found our seats; they were in the middle row of three. I had the aisle and Dan was in the middle, which was something I was to regret later on.

"Mate, I've got to go to the bathroom," he whispered, for the second time just after taking off.

"Are you fucking serious? You just went."

"Yeah, I need to fart."

"Every time you go, I've got to pause my movie and unplug my headphones, it's a fucking pain."

"Oh, I'm sorry, sweetheart, how about I just fart here."

"You're just skin covering a fart right now, aren't you?"

"Move!"

To make matters worse, there was an old Chinese bloke across the aisle to me who constantly wanted stuff out of his luggage. It was in the overhead compartment, so he kept getting out of his seat, opening the compartment to retrieve his bag, placing it on his seat, and then rummaging through it—each time, pushing his ass two inches from my face. Dan thought this was hilarious, and he kept elbowing me in the ribs to laugh at me.

After eight or so hours of Dan's relentless fart breaks and an incessant fifty-year-old ass in my face, we finally made it to Hong Kong International Airport. There we had an hour stop-over before heading on to Bangkok. Dan was desperate as all hell for a cigarette, so the security check we had to go through was most inconvenient for him. It also didn't help that I got pulled aside because a bottle of cologne I had was too large to be carrying on as hand luggage and, even though security threw my cologne into a bin, Dan was more pissed off than I was. "Who the fuck brings a bottle of cologne to Thailand? And not just any bottle but the biggest fucking bottle in the world."

"That was my favorite fucking cologne . . . they threw it in the bin!"

"Dude, seriously. We're going to a beach. You don't need cologne."

"It's okay," I sighed, "I've got a smaller bottle with me."

Dan couldn't help but laugh. "Jesus, dude, do you even have a cock?"

When we neared our gate, we saw smoking room after smoking room. Dan broke into a sprint to the nearest one. I thought to myself, if only Dan put as much energy into sport as he did smoking, he could've made a damn fine athlete. I passed by the smoking room and spied Dan already half-way through his first of many cigarettes. I can honestly say there is nothing more depressing on earth than the smoky confines of those rooms. It's a dreary bunch of gray-looking people standing around, puffing their lives away. Not talking, just staring into the distance, quietly shuffling their feet and probably wondering, when will it end? Seriously, if you smoke and want to quit, spend an hour in one of those things—they truly are hell on earth. Dan, on the other hand, loves them.

"How the fuck can you even go into those rooms? They're disgusting," I asked, when he found me at our gate.

"What do you mean? They're awesome. It's like I'm still smoking after I stop smoking. We're all literally smoking each other's ciggies."

"I reckon you could die in there if you sat in there long enough, like gassing yourself with car exhaust."

"Oh, definitely," he nodded.

"Yet you still go in there?"

"What's your point?"

I sat there waiting for Dan on numerous occasions while he smoked in that room. Even when the time came to board the plane, Dan was in there. I waved for him to come out, and he left reluctantly. "Come on, dude, let's go," I said when he returned.

"The line isn't even fucking moving."

"So?"

"I threw half a ciggie away."

"I'm just doing my bit to prolong your life, buddy." I put my arm around his shoulder.

"Piss off," he said giggling, and pushed my arm away. I pushed him back, and Dan grabbed me in a headlock.

"Passports, please," said a young lady from the airline, with a very stern look on her face.

"Sorry," I said, and handed her my passport.

"I was just giving him a wee cuddle," said Dan, as he handed over his too.

The young lady just gave him a look that said, "Like fuck you were."

We walked along the Jetway to board the plane, and I picked up a newspaper on the way. The headline read, "Two More Killed in Thai Riots," next to a picture of a guy throwing Molotov cocktails at a tank. "Holy shit, dude, look. There are tanks in the city killing people. I thought it was a demonstration not a fucking war." A certain group of Thais weren't too happy about the government at that time. They were demonstrating against the Prime Minister, calling for him to dissolve parliament and hold elections. Unfortunately, it had turned violent.

"Don't worry about it, dude; we'll be fine. They wouldn't fly us in if it were a war zone. Seriously, we'll look after each other." He placed a hand on my shoulder, which is about as affectionate as Dan gets.

"Yeah, you're probably right. I'm sure Laura and Flash would have warned us by now, eh?"

"Unless they've been injured in crossfire, of course."

"What?"

"Kidding, I'm kidding. We'll be fine."

The flight to Bangkok was just under three hours—during which Dan was suddenly hit with the urge to defecate, and Dan, being true to himself, had to do it at the most inopportune moment. Because, halfway through his moment of relief, the seatbelt sign came on, and the flight attendant warned us to return to our seats and prepare for landing. Dan, adhering to the rules on this one rare occasion, returned to his seat. "Dude, I wasn't finished, I had to break off," he said, as he sat down and buckled his seatbelt.

"What the fuck do you mean?"

"I hadn't finished shitting, so I had to break off halfway

through."

"Why didn't you finish?"

"The fucking seatbelt light came on."

"So? I'm pretty sure there's a grace period for people taking a dump, dude; you could've finished."

"Well, maybe that light should say, 'Return to your seat after you've finished your goddamned shit'."

Dan had to wait another 20 minutes before we landed, as well as the obligatory wait for first and business class to disembark. He sort of waddled like a duck to the nearest toilet while I waited outside with his wee bag. It was then I realized how hot it was, even inside the airport.

"It's fucking hot here, isn't it?" I said, as I handed Dan his wee bag on his return.

"It's Thailand, dickhead, what'd you expect, snow?"

"No, but Australia's hot too. This is just, hotter."

"We're in the airport, Myles, it's air-conditioned. Wait till we get outside, and then you can start talking about how fucking hot it is."

We strolled through Bangkok's magnificent Suvarnabhumi Airport to immigration, admiring various statues along the way. "You know, for some reason I thought we were going to arrive in a shithole, but this place is rather spectacular," I said, looking at a humongous statue of a purple-colored character with four arms, presumably a god.

"Yeah, it's probably one of the nicest airports I've ever been in."

"How many airports *have* you been in?"

"Three."

"You're a fucking idiot," I said, and we both cracked up laughing.

We reached immigration and joined a queue, but I didn't have long to wait before I was standing in front of a surly immigration officer with his hand out for my passport. I duly handed it to him, and he pointed at a little mug shot camera attached to his desk. He looked at my passport, and then at me for a little longer than I felt comfortable. He finally stamped it and, without so much as a word or a smile, he waved me through. I waited for Dan while he was put through the same 30 seconds of awkwardness, before we both headed to a lone, half-asleep customs officer leaning on an x-ray machine. I handed him my bag, but he just waved us through. "Fuck me, that was easy, eh?" I said.

"Yeah, I think it's the smuggling out, *and not in*, that they have a problem with, Myles. Either way, they shoot you, so I guess it's not much of a problem."

"Fair enough."

We followed signs that pointed the way to taxis, and then finally reached the automatic doors to outside. As soon as they opened, it was like I was hit in the face with a baseball bat made from a 40-degree, 100 percent humidity fart. My body instantly started sweating, and it was difficult to breathe. I panicked a little. "Holy shit, it's hot. I don't know if can handle this—and what the fuck is that smell?" I stammered.

Dan cracked up laughing. "You need to harden the fuck up, dude, because it's eight at night," he said, and calmly lit a cigarette. "Imagine what it's like in the middle of the day."

"How can you even smoke that in this heat?"

"Myles, I could smoke in the pits of hell."

"I honestly don't think this is far off."

"God, you're a pussy. Look, I guess we can get a cab over there, eh? Dan pointed to our left, where a crowd of people was milling around some taxis.

"Oh, okay. By the way, Flash told me we have to head to Khao San Road; they'll be waiting for us there. He also said that we shouldn't pay more than five hundred baht. We may have to haggle a bit."

"I think I can handle that, I'm pretty good at haggling."

"When the fuck have you ever haggled?"

"I haggle all the time. Being your friend is a constant haggle."

I sighed deeply, rolled my eyes, and walked over to a young lady who seemed to be coordinating the taxis. She politely said, "Welcome to Thailand, what is your destination?" in perfect English.

"Khao San Road, please," I said.

She waved a driver over and explained to him in Thai where we were going, which sounded a lot different than how I had said Khao San Road.

The taxi driver grabbed our bags, and we followed him to a bright pink taxi that had seen better years. I jumped into the back, and Dan took shotgun. The taxi driver couldn't speak a word of English, but Dan started the negotiations anyway. "How much to Khao San Road? Five hundred, right?"

"Dan, you're supposed to start lower," I tutted.

"Wha?" asked the driver.

"Khao San Road, five hundred baht?" Dan asked again.

"Khao San ah, fo hundret,"

"What? Four hundred?"

"Yah, fo hundret."

"Oh . . . okay, four hundred." Dan looked at me with a grin, and said, "That's how you do it, dickhead."

The taxi driver was weaving in and out of traffic like a madman. I looked over his shoulder at the speedometer; it read 130 kilometers. I quickly sat back in my seat and tried to relax. Dan tried to converse with the driver again. "How's your day been, mate?"

"Wha?"

"Your day, good?"

"Wha?"

"Day, your day?"

"Dan, shut the fuck up," I said.

As we drove along the motorway, humongous billboards advertising American fast-food brands and Japanese motor companies dotted the horizon, while high-rise apartments peeked over the barricade; makeshift clotheslines hung in every balcony.

When we finally reached downtown Bangkok, certain parts were blocked off because of the riots, and the streets overflowed with cars and tuk-tuks, which were beeping their horns incessantly. It was as though every car and tuk-tuk had an overexcited child at the wheel. We drove down a side street and stopped at the end of Khao San Road. We couldn't actually drive down the road itself because a huge market was in full swing. The smell was ten-times worse, and it was ten-times hotter, but we sucked it up and started walking down the road to find our hotel and Laura and Flash. Hundreds of stalls lined the street, selling everything from food, clothes, and shoes to sunglasses, ninja-stars, and butterfly knives. You could even buy fake press passes or drivers' licenses for any country in the world.

The market was packed with a mixture of travelers and Thais perusing the stalls or drinking and eating in the many restaurants or bars that spewed out onto the footpath. We also couldn't walk two steps without being accosted by street hawkers trying to sell us suits, tattoos, cigarette lighters, ping-pong sex shows or a myriad of other useless trinkets, bracelets, or toys. We walked the entire length of the road, trying to avoid them; a constant stream of rejections gushed from my mouth as we tried in vain to find Laura and Flash. "No, I don't want a tattoo. No, I don't want a suit, thanks. No, we don't need a taxi. No, thank you, I'm good for sex shows for now. No, like I've said to you before, I don't want a suit. It's 4,000 degrees, the last thing I want is a fucking suit."

Suddenly, through the ruckus, I heard, "Mylesie? Mylesie?"

I searched the faces till I saw Laura and Flash casually sitting at a small table enjoying a couple of cold beers, dressed in T-shirts and baggy Thai pants. It looked as though they had been there for years. "Hey, you finally made it?" said Laura, hugging the both of us when we reached them.

"I know, it's been quite the trip," I said. "Fuck it's hot, eh? And what the hell is that smell?"

"That, my friend, is the sweet, sweet smell of Thailand," said Flash, hugging the both of us too.

"Oh . . . kay," I said, unable to conjure up the same enthusiasm he seemed to have for it. "Look at the two of you, it's like you live here."

"Mate, we've been here before—we come well prepared."

"Check in there," said Laura, pointing directly behind her at a hotel. "And hurry up, we're starving."

As it turned out, our hotel, Rikka Inn, was about a third of the way down Khao San Road. It was clean and cheap, about 30 Australian for the one night, but the best thing of all, it was air-conditioned. Once I was in my room, I sucked large, deep breaths of the cold air deep into my lungs like I'd been starved of oxygen for the last hour, and then ran a cold shower. The last 13 hours disappeared down the drain, and a feeling of freedom came over my body as I changed into board shorts, jandals, and a fresh T-shirt. I stopped off at Dan's room on the way to grab him, and I noticed he was wearing the exact same outfit. "Have you showered?" I asked.

"Yes, why?"

"You're wearing the same clothes."

"Yeah, I know, remember? I've got to buy some shorts."

"Oh, yeah. Well, go and hurry up."

"It's okay, I'll do it later."

We met Laura and Flash again outside the hotel and, like me, Laura immediately focused on Dan's attire. "What the hell are you wearing, Dan?"

"I know, I know. I've got to buy some shorts,"

"You mean to say, you came to Thailand, one of the hottest countries in the world, without shorts?" said Flash.

"Or jandals," I chimed in, with a huge grin plastered over my face.

"What the hell were you thinking?" said Flash.

"What the fuck is this, the Thai fashion police? Look, I'll buy some later, all right? Let's just drink some piss."

We walked our way up Khao San Road and found a restaurant not far from our hotel for dinner. "So, how were your flights?" asked Laura.

"Not too bad. Having a stopover was hell, though," I said.

"Some old guy kept sticking his ass in Myles' face every five minutes. It was pure comedy gold for me," laughed Dan.

"You stuck your ass in my face every five minutes too, you prick."

"Myles, we both know you love my ass."

"Which one? You have two of them."

"What the fuck are you talking about?"

"You have another back ass, just above your other ass," I explained, pointing to the area above his bum, where he sported two love handles.

I constantly give Dan shit about being a little overweight, and by the same token, Dan constantly gives me shit about being a little underweight. "Well, that must make you insanely jealous, considering, you don't have an ass at all," he said.

"Piss off, I have an amazing bum," I said, turning around in my seat trying to look at my backside.

"What? Look at you. You resemble a martini garnish."

"A what?"

"A martini garnish, an olive on a toothpick . . ."

Luckily, Dan's food had arrived to stop the banter. There's something I should mention about Dan and his eating habits; he shovels food into his mouth faster than a starving dog. Seriously, he stops talking, puts his head down, and goes for it, with each spoonful refilled and in his mouth before the last is on its merry way down his throat. He'll devour a plate of food in about three minutes flat. He will then sit back and light up a cigarette. He couldn't care less if everyone else is still eating or not—he'll just light up and smoke. It's just so natural to him. It's like the smoke is oxygen, and he's doing you favor by blowing it into your face.

Since our food came at different times, as it does in Thailand—they don't bring it out all at once but stagger it, so we're all eating at different times—Flash copped a face full of Dan's smoke during his meal and coughed. "These smokes are killing me, I've got to give 'em up."

"Imagine how I feel," replied Dan, not realizing Flash's comment was sarcastic.

"Dan, go fucking smoke over there," I said, pointing to a lone table. This is a phrase I would come to repeat a million times over the next 14 days.

"Why?" he asked, genuinely confused.

"Seriously, bro, do I really need to tell you why?"

"It's okay, mate, just blow it in another direction," said Flash. "Come to think of it, how'd you go on the plane?"

"Oh my, God, dude, it was fucking terrible. I actually considered eating cigarettes for a while there. I also spent some time wondering if those toilet smoke alarms actually work, and if so, how many puffs I could get through before they tackled and arrested me."

"Dan made up for it by spending our whole Hong Kong layover in those smoking rooms," I added.

"Yeah, I smoked for Australia in Hong Kong."

"Smoking isn't a sport, Dan," said Laura.

"Well, it fucking well should be."

Once we had finished our meals, Flash spied a guy smoking a hookah pipe a few tables away. "Look, Dan, if you're going to smoke so much, why don't you smoke one of those? At the very least, it'll be easier on me," he said, coughing through a face full of Dan's Marlboro light.

Dan's eyes lit up like a Christmas tree.

"And we should probably get Sang Som bucket, since we're in Thailand and all," said Laura.

"Oh yeah, I've heard about those," I said.

"What's a Sang Som bucket?" asked Dan.

"It's a bucket of joy, Daniel," said Flash. "Put it this way, the last time I had a Sang Som bucket, I woke up on a beach, missing my wallet, passport, and all memory of the night before."

Dan didn't need to hear anymore. "One hookah, a Sang Som bucket, and four Singahs, please," he said, after waving a waitress over to our table.

Now the famous Sang Som bucket would prove to be Dan's archenemy—his kryptonite, so to speak. It's made in a small plastic bucket, similar to what a child would use to make sand castles at the beach. The bucket is filled with ice, a 300ml hip flask of Sang Som whiskey—they call it whiskey but it's actually rum—which is about 80 proof, a 150ml bottle of Red Bull syrup and a can of Coke. They're very sweet and you can't actually taste the whisky, so they're also very easy to drink. Most people, and Dan in particular, mistake them for a large cocktail and forget that they're actually drinking a whole hip flask of spirits and not just a few shots.

"Listen, guys," said Laura, "we need to discuss what you want to do from here. There's two ways we can get down to Surat Thani, which is where we need to go to catch the ferry to Koh Phangan."

"Yeah, we can either catch a train or bus. The train takes about nine to ten hours, the bus is about half an hour more," added Flash.

"Which is better?" I asked.

"Well, the train is more comfortable. They have bunks that you can sleep in all the way down," said Laura.

"Can you drink piss on the train?" asked Dan, taking a large sip from the Sang Som bucket.

"Yeah, of course you can. It's Thailand, Dan, you can drink piss wherever you want," said Flash.

"Well, let's get the train, then," I said.

"Cool. We'll get up early tomorrow and organize the train tickets and transfers. It should be about 250 baht each, if my memory serves me right," said Laura.

"Hey, what time is it? We've got to pick up Kimmy from the airport 1:00," I interrupted.

"Relax, Myles, we've got plenty of time," said Dan, as he ordered another Sam Song bucket.

He was right. I needed to relax; I was in Thailand, for Christ's sake. I took a hit of the hookah, a sip of the bucket, and sat back in my seat.

But Bangkok doesn't let you relax. It's moving a million miles an hour. People are everywhere drinking, yelling and screaming, beeping horns, arguing with one another, or trying to sell you something you don't need. The street hawkers are the most annoying. They're about as welcome as Jehovah's Witnesses knocking at your door. Ironically, like Jehovah's Witnesses, they come up to your table in a zombie-like state, even while you're eating, trying to sell bracelets, lighters, trinkets and other cheaply made things. A simple "No thank you" doesn't deter them at all. You need to be stern, maybe yell a bit and wave your hands, like you would to a dog trying to hump your leg.

Dan seemed to be a magnet for these people. He would graciously listen to their pitch, which was usually no more than one word repeated over and over again. He'd then look through their little tray, pulling each thing out, putting it against his wrist, or lighting the lighters. He would then put them all back and shake his head. Except, if you touch their stuff, that's as good as sold as far as they're concerned, and no amount of head shaking or hand waving will get rid of them. So, after an awkward stalemate on one particular occasion, Dan reluctantly bought five friendship bracelets, one of which he gave to me, Laura and Flash. We all put them on, since it was a nice gesture, and cheered our drinks.

A few hours, two Sang Som buckets, and countless beers had Laura and Flash turning in. Dan decided midnight was a perfectly normal time to go clothes-shopping, and, as a result, we started perusing a few of the last remaining stalls on Khao San Road for shorts and appropriate footwear. As it turns out, board shorts made from quick-dry material were slightly more expensive than their cotton counterparts, and when I say slightly, I mean like a dollar. Dan thought this was a good enough reason not to buy board shorts, so he just bought shorts. He also decided it was better to buy more shoes rather than open footwear.

"You do realize we're going to a beach, for two weeks, don't you?" I said, as we walked back to our hotel.

"Yeah, why?"

"You'll need board shorts to swim in and fucking jandals."

"Board shorts were thirty bucks more expensive."

"Thirty baht, Dan, thirty baht—which is a fucking dollar, by the way. And don't get me started on the fucking shoes you just bought. We're going to the beach. Why won't you buy jandals—or any open footwear, for that matter?"

"I'll just buy that shit once we get down there."

"Buy them now. Look, I'll buy them for you, my treat."

"Why the fuck do you care so much?"

"Fuck knows. Maybe it's because you make me feel like I need to mother you, or maybe it's because you're a frustrating cunt. But, what I do know is, you're going to need jandals, because you can't wear fucking shoes *on a beach*."

"But . . . jandals don't suit me," he finally confessed.

"What the fuck are you talking about, how can they not suit you? You can hardly see them."

"I don't know. I've just never been one to wear them is all."

"Then, how do you know if they suit you or not?

"Who fucking cares, dude, seriously? We'll be on sand, won't we? I'll go barefoot."

I sighed and rubbed my brow. "Go and change, and hurry the fuck up. We've got to get Kimmy."

Dan changed into his new shorts and shoes, and then we set out to negotiate the price to pick up Kimmy. After witnessing Dan's amazing haggling once again, we managed to settle on 1,000 baht round-trip, which, according to my calculations, was 200 more than our last taxi ride, but we set off to collect Kimmy anyway.

When we got there, the driver parked in the parking lot and came with us to the gate. I thought he was scared we were going do a runner, but Dan insisted it was what the extra 200 baht was paying for.

Kimmy finally appeared through the crowd, and a huge grin spread over her face as she spied us at the gate waving like a couple of adolescent kids at a Santa parade.

"Hey, how are you doing?" she said, hugging and kissing the both of us. "Man, it's hot."

"Oh, don't talk to Myles about the heat. It seems he's very sensitive to hot weather," said Dan, handing her the last of the bracelets he'd bought earlier.

"Cool," she said, and started tying it on her wrist. "What's that smell?"

"Oh, and the odor is a touchy subject, too," giggled Dan, helping her with the bracelet.

"Get fucked, Dan," I said, and reached for Kimmy's bag, which was rather large for traipsing around beaches. "Jesus, Kimmy, is you're bag big enough? What's in there?"

"Bikinis."

"How many, a thousand?" I started lifting her bag up and down feeling the weight of it, which—again—was too heavy for traipsing around beaches.

"Myles, I'm a girl."

"Don't worry about it, Kimmy. He gave me shit about my bag, too," said Dan, as we followed the taxi driver back to his cab. "He's very particular about the size of luggage, for some reason. It's either too small or too big, wear this or wear that." He sighed, and gave me a smirk. "She's a hard road trying to be as perfect as Myles."

Kimmy and Dan both laughed.

"All right, all right. Shut it, you prick," I said, giving in and laughing with them.

Fifteen minutes and another death-defying ride later, we were back on Khao San Road. We checked Kimmy in at the hotel, and it was there we decided that she would stay with me for the first night, since it was too late to book another room. We would then get our own rooms once we were down in Koh Phangan.

Kimmy quickly freshened up, and we headed back out on the road. The market was completely packed away as we sat down at a bar called Lucky Beer. Dan immediately bought another Sang Som bucket with a round of beer. It was quite the party atmosphere; every table was talking to each other, and, as it turned out, a bunch of New Zealanders were next to us. So, we all got on as we drank beers and buckets, every now and again raising our drinks with them over an irrelevant event or a friend of theirs who was, at that moment, having a birthday in another country.

During one conversation, or rather friendly debate, with one of the Kiwis about the current New Zealand rugby team, Kimmy elbowed me in the ribs and said, "I think you need to take a look at Dan."

Dan had appeared at the table with a rather large woman who looked a lot like a man. People had warned us prior to coming about the lady-boys in Thailand, but lady-boys are actually pretty boys who look like pretty girls, and this woman was a not-so-pretty woman who looked like an even uglier man.

"Uh-oh. Err, Dan, what are you doing?" I asked.

"Hey, this is my new friend," he said, with a huge grin on his face, and eyes that weren't really cooperating with his brain. The woman didn't bother to acknowledge any of us as they both sat down.

"I've got to get a photo of this," said Kimmy, grabbing her

camera. She asked the both of them to smile and took a photo.

Dan's new friend must have thought she was the Angelina Jolie of Thailand, because she took great offense and started yelling, "Delete! Delete! Delete!" The rest of us stared in bewilderment. She abruptly stood up, yelled something in Thai, and then left for another table.

"What . . . the . . . fuck was that all about, Dan?" I asked, once she was gone.

"Dunno," he said, shrugging.

"There's something seriously dodgy about her, Dan. I think you should stay away . . . " Dan didn't bother to listen. He got up and went inside, only to return with another bucket and a round of beers.

"Whoa, dude. After this one, I'm going to bed," I said, holding up the bottle of beer I was already drinking. "It's three thirty in the morning, and we've got to travel for ten hours tomorrow."

"Yeah, Dan, I'm pretty tired, too," said Kimmy, agreeing with me.

"Don't be such pussies," he said, putting the drinks down in front of us. "We're on holiday, for fuck's sake."

We both sighed but obliged, and drank the beers but skipped on the bucket. Not long after, Dan disappeared, only to return with the ugly woman again. "Jesus Christ, what the fuck is he doing?" I whispered to Kimmy.

"I don't know. He's your friend."

"Dan, we're going back to the hotel. Let's go," I yelled, getting up from the table.

Dan looked up at me with a look of disgust. "What? You're going?"

"*We're* going, all three of us. Let's go."

"Who the fuck do you think you are, my dad? I'm staying.

Kimmy, you're not going, are you?"

"Yeah, I'm so tired I need to sleep, and I really think you should come too."

"Fuck that. I'll see you pussies in the morning then."

I pulled one of our Kiwi friends aside and asked, "Bro, can you keep an eye on our mate over there? He's wasted, and he's been awake for well over 24 hours."

"Yeah, no worries, bro. He's sweet with us. Why don't you stay? We'll probably kick on somewhere else soon."

"Nah, we're tired. It was nice to meet you, though, brother."

"Sure, see you . . . " was all I cared to hear from our Kiwi friend as Kimmy and I walked back to our air-conditioned room.

As soon as my head hit the pillow, I was asleep. I too had been awake for over 24 hours.

Smell Your Dick

We awoke the next morning to a knocking at our door, "Hey, do you want to get breakfast?" yelled Flash, from the other side.

My head was throbbing, and I felt like I could probably sleep for another six or so months, but breakfast seemed like the perfect alternative. "Sure, we'll be right out," I yelled back.

I quickly showered, got dressed, and, while Kimmy was getting ready, went across the hall to Dan's room and banged on his door. There was no response. I returned to my room and rang his on the landline, but still no response. I tried his mobile, but that went straight to voice mail.

"Fuck, I can't get hold of Dan. I hope he's okay," I said to Kimmy.

"He'll be all right. Maybe he's already outside with the others."

Once Kimmy had finished getting ready, we met Laura and

Flash out front of the hotel, but Dan wasn't with them. So, after Laura, Flash and Kimmy were done hugging, I asked, "Hey, have you guys seen Dan?"

"No, did you knock on his door?" said Laura.

"Yeah, I've rung him too, but I can't get hold of him."

Flash shook his head and chuckled, "What the fuck happened last night?"

Kimmy and I explained as best as we could about the night: the bar, the buckets, and the ugly woman or man, for all we knew. Kimmy also showed them the photo of Dan and his friend.

"Holy shit," said Flash. "He's probably lying in a gutter somewhere."

"Or a bathtub filled with ice with his kidneys removed," I chortled.

"Don't be mean. He's probably gone to check out a temple, or something," said Kimmy.

"There is no way in hell Dan would have gotten up early to visit a temple. You saw the state he was in. He's probably spooning with that chick-slash-dude right now."

"If he was as drunk as you say he was, then he's probably still passed out," said Flash.

"Well, maybe we should check the police station," said Laura, genuinely concerned.

"Yeah, you're probably right. Look, after breakfast we'll get someone from the hotel to open his door, and if he's not there, we'll check the police station. But knowing Dan, I'm sure he's only just got to bed and is sleeping it off. In fact, I wouldn't be surprised if we see him still at that bar, drinking, when we walk past."

We chose a place a little out of the way for breakfast, during which Laura shared a little bit of wisdom about eating abroad. "If you drink a Coke with every meal, it sort of safeguards you against getting diarrhea."

"How?" I asked.

"I don't know; someone told me about it when we were traveling."

"Does it work?" asked Kimmy.

"So far it has for us—well, for me anyway, eh, babe?" said Laura with a cheeky grin.

"What does she mean?" I asked Flash.

"That's a story for when we're not eating, trust me. Anyway, we got up early to book our train tickets to Surat Thani, but the train was booked solid. We're going to have to take the bus instead. It leaves at 9:00 tonight, so we have the day to get supplies for the beach."

"Yeah, you're going to want to get a sarong and a hammock, along with anything else you need," added Laura. "The sarong doubles as a beach towel so you don't have to lug one around.

"Jesus, Laura, you're like a walking Lonely Planet, aren't you?" I said.

After breakfast, we wandered around downtown Bangkok; it was a lot busier than the night before, but with fewer travelers and more locals. Cars and tuk-tuks were speeding around, beeping as always; it was organized chaos, or maybe just chaos that was functioning on pure luck. They actually have big LED signs above their traffic lights that count down the red and green lights, so you can time running the red and jumping the green to perfection.

I popped into a pharmacy to inquire about drugs. Flash told me you could procure anything you want in Thailand without a prescription. He said, "The first time I ever came to Thailand, I came with a mate of mine, Lloyd. He took me to a pharmacy to buy Temazepam. I thought he'd probably just grab a few for all the traveling we'd be doing. Lloyd bought forty of them.

"Anyway, one night while we were sitting at our resort bar in Koh Samui, Lloyd thought it a good idea to take a couple and drink Sang Som buckets. He turned it into a competition to see who could stay awake the longest. The thinking was that the Red Bull in the buckets would keep us awake. It didn't. When I woke up the next morning, I was lying on the sand in the middle of the beach with my wallet and passport gone. When I went back to our resort bar and asked the old lady if she'd seen it, she said, 'You crazy boys. You go to sleep on beach an' I fine wallet an' paport near bungalow. An' you' friend! You' friend, he talk all night long, keep me wake all night, not good, not good.' Which meant Lloyd bloody won."

At the pharmacy, I put in an order for sleeping pills and painkillers. Amazingly, just as Flash had explained, they grabbed a big cookie tin filled with pills and poured however many I wanted into little plastic bags, which, in turn, made it look like the drugs were illicit—in retrospect, they probably were.

When we reached Khao San Road, Kimmy and I bought our mandatory sarongs and hammocks. Then, as we approached the hotel, I heard my name called in a very high-pitched voice. I scanned the crowd to finally see Dan emerge, wide-eyed and very pale, yet sweating considerably. He was in the same clothes he'd been wearing the night before, and he embraced me, which was very unlike Dan. This instantly concerned us all.

He stammered into my shoulder, "Dude, I've been looking everywhere for you. Where have you been?"

"We were at breakfast. Are you okay?"

"You wouldn't believe what happened to me last night.

Jesus Christ, I can't stop shaking."

He was talking a millions miles an hour, he looked terrible, and he really was shaking. "Calm down, bro," I said, "take a seat and breathe. It's fine. We're all here now."

I sat him down at the closest bar. "Now tell us what happened." Before he could say anything, a waitress appeared, so we obliged and ordered a pint each. Dan, still shaking, tried to order a Sang Som bucket.

"Whoa, dude!" I said, putting my hand over his mouth. "No, he'll have a beer too, please," I said to the waitress. "Dan, I think they're the reason you're in this mess. Now, tell us from the start, what the fuck happened?"

He lit a cigarette and, after taking a few long, hard puffs, he calmed down enough to tell us. "God, I'm glad to see you guys. I can't remember a fucking thing from last night—pretty much after we picked you up, Kimmy. It's all just blank." He puffed on his cigarette again with a shaking hand before continuing. "I woke up this morning, naked, in a filthy apartment. As you can imagine, I freaked the fuck out." Again, Dan paused to drag hard on his cigarette, almost finishing it. "And then, as I was trying to figure out what the hell was going on, this fucking ugly chick walked out from the bathroom, naked, and said, 'Helloooo'." Dan said this in a very bad Thai accent. "I asked her what happened the night before, and she said, 'We have very nice sex.' Nice sex? With me? I knew she was lying. I yelled, 'No we fucking didn't!' and put my clothes on as quickly as I could.

"I checked my wallet, and my bloody ATM card was gone. I thought, thank Christ, I've just been robbed and not had sex. When I asked her where my card was, she said, 'What card?' so I yelled, 'Fuck!' and ran out of there. I must have been drugged. The weird thing was, I still had a little cash in my wallet, so I was able to get a taxi back."

We sat there with our mouths open, unable to speak, trying to process what he had just told us. Dan looked up at each of us from the corners of his eyes, like he was about to burst into tears and puffed vigorously on another cigarette.

"Holy fucking shit," said Flash, finally breaking the silence.

"Have you checked your bank account?" asked Laura.

"Yeah, there's a transaction for 800 dollars. It's the most you can get out on my card in a 24-hour period. I need to cancel it before midnight, but I can't seem to get through to the bank on my phone."

"Holy fucking shit," repeated Flash.

"I've been trying your phone all morning, but it's going straight to voice mail," I said. "What's the number? I'll try on my phone." I called his bank for him, and we managed to cancel his card so nothing else could be taken.

"So, did you actually have sex?" asked Kimmy.

"I can't remember a thing, so I don't really know. I'm freaking out about contracting something." Dan paused to drag his cigarette, while his mind probably ticked over the potential diseases that he may have contracted. "What if I have AIDS? I heard it's rife here."

"If she was the same one that we saw, then she was way too fat to have AIDS," I said.

"You're not helping, Myles."

"Did she have a cock?" asked Flash.

"No, I don't think so. I think she was just an ugly chick."

"I guess one way you can tell if you had sex is to smell your dick. If it smells of vagina, then you probably had sex," I explained.

Dan stuck his hand down his pants, wriggled it around a bit then pulled it out and smelt it. He shook his head and shoved his hand toward my face.

"Oh my God, gross!" cried Kimmy.

"Dude, I'll take your word for it," I said, quickly pulling away. "That rules out vaginal sex, but you can't rule out anal rape. Is your ass sore?"

"I wasn't anally raped, dickhead."

"Hey, Kimmy, show him the photo that you showed us this morning," said Laura.

Kimmy showed him the damning photo that she had taken of the girl Dan had been sitting with.

"Yeah, that's her," he said.

"Him," said Flash, trying hard to hide his ever-growing urge not to laugh.

"Who was she? I don't remember any of that."

"I'll be fucked if I know. You found her somewhere and appeared at our table with her," I said.

"Why didn't you warn me?"

"We did! But you must have the best fucking beer goggles in the world. We actually got rid of her at one stage."

"What happened?"

"You went and got her again! Then you wouldn't come home when I asked. Even Kimmy tried."

Kimmy nodded. Flash couldn't contain it any longer and burst out laughing, Dan started looking sicker. I smiled and patted him on the shoulder. "Look, bro, I'm sure you're okay. I'll lend you as much cash as you need, so you don't have to worry about that, okay?" Dan nodded and lit another cigarette.

Later, when our holiday was over and we were back in Sydney, Dan and I read, on the Internet, about a scam in Thailand and other parts of the world, where people befriend you, and then spike your drink with a drug called Scopolamine. The CIA used it as a truth serum in the sixties. There have been many reports of people being held on this stuff for days, while their accounts are drained dry.

When Dan and I discussed this being what could have happened to him, he vaguely recalled someone asking him for his pin number, and, at the time, he had assumed it was me.

Once Dan calmed down, we moved to a restaurant to get a meal into him while the rest of us enjoyed a few more beers. "Dan, what flavor beer do you want?" I asked, as he quietly shoveled spoonful after spoonful of some sort of fluorescent red goo into his mouth.

"I'm over beer," he spat, "anything but." Dan picked up the menu and scanned the cocktail section while sucking goo from the gaps in his teeth. "Mai tai. I'll have a mai tai," he finally said, then went back to shoveling the red goo into his gob.

"Four beers and a mai tai for the princess, please." I politely asked the waitress.

When our drinks arrived, Dan eagerly sucked down the cocktail before the waitress had even finished putting the rest of our beers down. "Fuck, that was good," he said with a sigh of contentment, "I'll have another, please." And he did, and another. He drank two, nearly three mai tais to everyone else's one beer, and it wasn't long before he was drunk again. With every drink, he got less concerned about what had just happened to him, and more fascinated about the array of useless goodies he could buy from the street hawkers. The more trinkets he looked at, the more hawkers he attracted. It was as though Dan had decided that the Thai useless-shit market was in some sort of jeopardy, and that he would take it upon himself to singlehandedly save it. He bought a ridiculously large lighter, a myriad of different bracelets, four cigars, and a photo with a live iguana sitting on his shoulder. Dan went through 2,000 baht in about an hour with all his cocktails and trinkets.

"Dan, stop wasting money on rubbish. You need to get a hammock and sarong for the beach," I said, starting to get impatient.

"A sarong? When did your cock shrivel up into a vagina, Myles?" he said, laughing hysterically, and then, shaking his head, he repeated, "A sarong."

"No, Dan, it's for lying on the beach instead of a towel. They're easier to carry than towels," explained Laura.

"Oh, I'm sorry. So, it's to prevent your flaps from getting sandy then, Myles?"

I couldn't help but laugh. "Get a sarong and a hammock, or you'll regret it," I said, trying my best to sound stern.

However, Dan ignored me. "Look at this ridiculously huge lighter, would you? I can't wait for someone to ask me for a light. I can pull it out, and say, 'Why yes, I do, sir—only the biggest fucking lighter you've ever seen'." Dan started pulling it from his hip and lighting it, like he was the fastest lighter in the Wild West.

"Wouldn't it be awesome if someone had one of those massive Cuban cigars and asked you for a light?" laughed Flash.

"Then my life would be complete, Flash."

"Come on," interrupted Laura, "we've got two hours before we have to catch the bus."

We checked out of the hotel and headed next door to an Irish bar called Mulligan's for dinner and to wait for a guide who was supposed to take us to our bus. We ordered some food, and Dan ordered a few more cocktails. Then, with 20 minutes to go, Dan suddenly blurted, "I want to go get a tattoo."

Just like that—out of the blue, no warning—he just decides he wants to get a tattoo. "You're fucking kidding, right?" I said.

"No! Come on, let's do this. It won't take long. It's on my list of things to do here."

"What fucking list?"

"I've got a list in my head of a bunch of things to do or buy while I'm here in Thailand."

"Was getting drugged and fucked in the ass by a she-male on that list? Because you can put a big fucking tick next to that."

"You don't have time to get a tattoo, Dan," pleaded Laura. "We're leaving in less than 20 minutes."

"Well, I'll get a piercing then."

"Piercing, what do want to get pierced?" asked Kimmy.

"My nose."

"Jesus Christ," sighed Flash, shaking his head and starting to look weary of it all.

"What is this, 1985? No one gets their nose pierced anymore, you Muppet," I said, desperately trying to put him off.

"Dude, look at this nose. It's perfect! It's probably my best quality. A nose ring will only accentuate how truly buttony it is."

"Buttony? What the fuck are you talking about? That's not even a word."

"Kimmy, do you want to come with me to get my nose pierced?"

"Sure!"

"You'll have to hurry. Go right now; you've got 15 minutes to get it done and back here for the bus," said Laura.

"I can't believe this is happening." I said, as I followed Dan and Kimmy out the door. We ran down Khao San and up the stairs of the nearest tattoo parlor. Unfortunately they didn't do piercings, but one of the tattooists knew of a place and offered to take us. We followed him over Khao San and down a very dimly lit alleyway. As we turned corners, the walls got tighter and darker. We passed a homeless guy sleeping in the shadows, and I thought to myself, great, Dan's going to get us bloody robbed and murdered for our troubles. But thankfully, we came back out onto a busy street right by another tattoo parlor. We thanked our guide and piled inside.

Bright fluorescent lights lit up the shop, except for one that flickered on and off in the corner. The walls were plastered with drawings and photos of tattoos and, for all intents and purposes, it looked clean and sanitary. Dan approached a heavily tattooed Thai guy behind a cabinet that housed a horde of different tattoo guns for sale. "I'd like my nose pierced please," he said, almost childlike, as if he were buying an ice cream.

The guy grinned a row of gold teeth, and then led Dan into a room out the back. Kimmy and I found an old couch to wait on, and started skimming through the many tattoo portfolios and magazines that were strewn over a coffee table. "I can't believe he is actually going through with this. Getting his fucking nose pierced after a two-second decision," I said to Kimmy.

"And while drunk," she added.

"I wonder whether the date-rape drugs are playing a part in this?"

"Hmm. I wonder if it'll get infected? I mean, we are going to a beach."

"Probably. In fact, of course it will, it's Dan."

Five minutes passed, then Dan emerged from the backroom with a silver ring looped through his left nostril.

"Oh my God, Dan, that's the gay side," said Kimmy.

"What?"

Kimmy and I laughed. "I'm kidding," she said, "did it hurt?"

"A wee bit. Does it look good?"

"Not at all, actually," I said.

"Whatever, dickhead. Kimmy, what do you think?"

"Um . . . I think it accentuates your very buttony nose."

"Thank you, Kimmy."

"Come on, Boy George, let's go. We've got a bus to catch," I said.

We raced back to the bar to retrieve our gear and meet up with Laura and Flash.

"Holy shit. I can't believe you just did that," said Laura, when she saw Dan's piercing.

"You're fucking crazy, man," laughed Flash.

"Kimmy said it accentuates my nose," said Dan, showing it off.

"Yep, It definitely accentuates something," said Flash, still laughing.

At that very moment, a young Thai guy greeted us. He asked if we were catching the bus, and if so, we should follow him. We grabbed our luggage and set off down Khao San Road toward the bus.

Along the way, the guide stopped a few times to collect other travelers who were heading to Surat Thani as well. The second time this happened, an old man selling hammocks accosted Dan in the street. I thought, word must've got 'round that Dan was in town to prop up the useless-shit trade. The hammocks were different from the ones we all had; they were made out of a lot of strands of cotton, bunched together and tied in a large diamond pattern. They didn't look very comfortable at all.

"Don't buy that, Dan," I sighed, "it looks dodgy."

Dan ignored me and bought it anyway, probably out of spite more than anything. "Here's ya bloody hammock, Myles. Happy now?"

"It's a shit hammock, you cock. You're going to hate it."

"It's just a hammock; they're all the same. Christ, what is it with you? I've got to have the right bag, footwear, shorts, and now a fucking hammock."

"Fine, I'm done helping you."

All the way to the bus, Dan continued to be annoyingly loud. "Why the fuck are we walking? Why don't we get a cab? Let's get a fucking tuk-tuk," he yelled, and pointed at a tuk-tuk across the road. He then yelled, "Tuk-tuk! Tuk-tuk! Tuk-tuk!" and pumped his fist in the air. "Come on, it'll be fun. Does this guy even know where the fuck he's going? Where the fuck are we going?"

"Dan, shut the fuck up," I yelled, losing my patience.

"Oh, my God, we've got ten hours of this," said Laura.

The bus looked rather old and rundown when we finally reached it. Kind of like that piece of shit your city council would keep running for an extra ten years to save money, and it would turn up every time you had to catch the bus even though all you've been seeing is fancy new ones every other day.

"That doesn't look too comfy, bro," I whispered to Flash.

"I hear ya. The last time we took this trip, it was a lot nicer than this heap."

We reluctantly handed our bags to the driver, and, as he swung them into the storage area below, we walked up the steps onto the bus. The first thing I noticed was the heat; it was almost twice as hot as outside. Most of the seats at the front were taken, and the farther back we got, the hotter it got. Laura and Flash found two empty seats, and then Dan grabbed two opposite the aisle to them. I grabbed the seats right behind Laura and Flash, and Kimmy sat next to me.

"Would you like to come and sit with me, Kimstar?" said Dan, in a childlike voice, all of a sudden giving Kimmy a new nickname.

"Thanks, Dan, but I'm okay here."

I tried to get comfortable and noticed the lack of air coming from the wee hole above my seat.

"Fuck, it's hot," I said, "and I've got no air at all."

"It's only going to get hotter because we're sitting above the engine," said Flash.

"Maybe it'll work once we get going," said Laura, optimistically.

But it didn't, and it did get hotter because of the engine. "Fuck this," said Flash, and got up to speak to the driver.

Kimmy discovered a lever that made the seats recline. "Cool—at least we can sleep properly."

"Oh, we'll sleep all right. I've got those sleeping pills with me," I said, holding up my bag of tablets.

"Even better!"

Flash returned to his seat with some bad news, "Apparently it's the best that they can do; the air-conditioning is fucked."

We all cursed in our own way, slumped back into our seats, and tried our very best to get comfortable. Before we left the city, we stopped a couple of times to pick up more travelers.

"Is this the train station? I can't see it," said Dan, looking out the window on the first occasion.

"What are you on about? We're just picking up more people," I said.

"I can't take this fucking heat," he moaned. "I wish this would hurry up. How far away is the train station?"

"Holy shit, we totally forgot. Dan has no idea we're on the bus all the way down," said Laura quietly to Flash, Kimmy and me. Dan had been absent when Flash had told us about the train being booked out and, with all the excitement of his supposed rape, we had forgotten to tell him. So he was under the impression the bus was just transport to the train station.

"Oh, fuck," whispered Flash, looking over at Dan as he

pressed his face and torso up against the window trying to cool off.

"I know. He's going to shit bricks when he finds out," I said, barely able to contain my grin.

The bus stopped again. "Oh, no, it's the bloody train station," said Flash, looking out the window.

Except, Dan saw it too. "Is this it? Come on, let's get off this fucking thing," he said, and started to get out of his seat.

"No, Dan, were not getting off the bus just yet," said Laura sternly.

"Why not? When do we get off?"

"This is it, mate. We're taking the bus all the way down," said Flash.

"You mean we're on this piece of shit for what? Six hours?" A look of fear spread across his face.

"Um. Try eight," said Flash.

"Eight?"

"I thought it was ten?" I asked.

"Yeah, it is. I just didn't want to freak him out too much."

"Oops," I said, giving Dan a sly smile.

"Ten?" Dan slumped back into his seat and stared into the back of the chair in front, biting his nails. He finally said, "Why the fuck did we sit back here by the toilet? It stinks of piss and shit."

"There weren't any seats up front, you fucking idiot," I said, getting annoyed again. "You just walked past them, remember?"

"Why did you let me drink all of those cocktails, then? You bastards."

"Dan, seriously? You didn't listen to anything we tried to tell you today," said Laura.

"I bought a hammock, didn't I?"

Dan sat back down into his seat and tried to get comfortable, but I knew he would suffer. The heat and smell was madness. It smelled as though every time somebody had used that toilet, they'd had a severe bout of dysentery, and it had never been emptied or cleaned—not in a hundred years. Needless to say, I couldn't take it either. I took a sleeping pill and offered them to Laura, Flash and Kimmy, but Laura and Flash abstained. I didn't offer them to Dan; half of me wanted him to suffer for ignoring me and being annoying all day, while the other half was worried about what he had in his system from when his drink was spiked. Within 15 minutes, Kimmy and I were both out, fast asleep.

I vaguely remember waking for a pit stop. I have absolutely no idea what time it was, but it was like a dream because of the sleeping pill. We were at some sort of eatery, and the other travelers were off the bus buying food. I left Kimmy sleeping and walked off the bus to investigate. The only lights in the pitch-black night were illuminating the shop. I imagined we were in the middle of space and this was a floating café. If I stepped off the edge, I would be gone, floating off into the darkness forever.

I had a look at the food, but it didn't look at all appetizing. In fact, I didn't even feel like walking let alone eating, so I sort of floated back toward the bus. At one point, Flash tapped me on the shoulder and, grinning, pointed at a window on the bus. It was completely covered in condensation apart from two feet pressed against the glass at the very top—Dan's feet. As I got back on the bus, I had to slide around Dan's head because it protruded out into the aisle. He looked mighty uncomfortable, as he was lying across the seats with his legs on a ninety-degree angle up against the glass. I wondered, why doesn't he just re-cline the seat back like everyone else? I slumped back into my seat next to Kimmy and immediately fell asleep.

When the bus finally reached Surat Thani, we had an hour's wait before the ferry arrived to take us to Koh Phangan. Kimmy and I were still really dopey from the pills, so we continued to sleep in a rough makeshift shelter, with most of the other travelers lying on the ground with our bags as pillows.

When the ferry did arrive, I vaguely remember Kimmy and I both walking on in a zombie-like state. We immediately slumped together on some seats and passed out again. God bless sleeping pills.

The Fucking Seats Reclined?

When I awoke, it took more than a few minutes to figure out exactly where I was. I woke Kimmy, who was nestled into my shoulder, and she too looked a little confused—I wasn't sure if it was because of the sleeping pills or the fact that we were cuddling.

We got up and ventured outside to find the others. It was an incredible day: not a cloud in the sky, and hot. Laura, Flash, and Dan were sitting on the top deck with their legs over the side of the boat. "Hey, how are we all feeling?" I said, once we reached them.

"Not too bad, now that we're off that fucking bus," said Flash.

"Yeah, that was absolute hell," said Laura.

Dan didn't say a word; he just stared at the sea splashing on the side of the boat.

"Really? I feel pretty good," I said, deeply breathing in the ocean air. "I'm glad those seats reclined."

"What? The fucking seats reclined?" said Dan finally rousing. "That was the most uncomfortable ten hours of my life. No bastard told me the fucking seats reclined."

"Settle down, bro. I thought you'd have worked it out for yourself. All you had to do was look around—the whole fucking bus was reclined in their seats."

"No, I didn't work it out. How far did they go back?"

"Not that far to be honest, not that it mattered anyway; that sleeping pill knocked me clean out. I hardly even remember the bus ride."

"You had sleeping pills? You bastard! When the fuck did you buy sleeping pills, and where was mine?"

"I bought them when you were spooning with your boyfriend. And to be totally honest, I didn't think it was a very good idea to give one to you since your rape. Who knows what you've got in your system?"

"Do you know how fucking uncomfortable I was on that bus?"

"Yeah, yeah, so you keep saying."

"I literally slept in the aisle at one stage. And, for the record, I didn't get raped."

"Well, since you can neither deny nor confirm sexual intercourse, I'm going to assume there was a rape." I giggled, but Dan didn't. He wasn't in the mood for jokes. He didn't look too good either, and the longer we were on the boat, the sicker he looked.

"Dan, are you okay? You're not seasick, are you?" asked Kimmy, sounding genuinely concerned.

"Yeah, mate, you're a little green around the gills," said Flash.

Dan didn't respond; he just continued to stare at the waves.

"I was seasick once," I said, "I had been drinking the night

68

before, and we went fishing early in the morning for a stag do. I was fine till we hit the open sea, and then it started." I made a noise like I was vomiting. "And I didn't stop spewing till I was on dry . . . " Before I could finish, Dan leapt to his feet and ran down the stairs to the toilet.

Kimmy tutted. "Myles! Look what you've done."

"Fuck. I hope he's all right," I said, trying my best to sound sincere.

When he eventually returned, he was disoriented and tripped a couple of times on the decking. His face was whitish gray, and he was sweating profusely. "Jesus, mate, you look terrible," said Flash.

"Oh, really? You know . . . it might be because I just spewed the entire contents of my stomach, including the lining, into the toilet downstairs," he stammered.

"Shit, stomach lining too, huh?"

"Yeah, because the whole time I was spewing, I was staring at and breathing in all the piss and shit at the bottom of the hole. So, it kept me spewing after my initial spew."

"Dan, you're on a boat, why didn't you just stay where you were, and go over the side?" I asked.

"I don't think the rest of us would have liked that, Myles," said Laura.

"Oh yeah, good point."

"Don't worry, I'm sure there's an encore coming shortly," said Dan.

"Dude, go and lie down in the middle of the boat, on your back, and close your eyes. It won't stop the sickness, but it should stop you from vomiting. That's the only thing that seemed to work for me the last time I had it. Fuck that 'stare at the horizon' bullshit—that just makes it worse."

"It was your story about last time you had it that did this to me, you bastard."

"Whoa, I can't take all the blame. You did drink a ridiculous amount of alcohol yesterday, not to mention the drugs you ingested before you were raped."

"I wasn't fucking . . . ah fuck it." Dan didn't have the energy to engage in any banter; he shuffled away and found some space in the middle of the boat and quietly lay down on his back. He was only wearing shorts, so the 40-degree sun lit up his torso so brightly that when I closed my eyes, there were red copies of Dan burnt into my eyelids. Dan also wears his pants ridiculously low, like he's unsure as to where his waist actually is, which meant most of his body was exposed to the sunlight.

Our ferry ride was long but cathartic; it was such a relief to be out of the city and on the ocean. The sea was a beautiful deep blue, and the smell of piss and shit had been replaced with briny sea air. Bliss.

When we docked at Koh Phangan, the wharf was overflowing with people screaming and waving signs at us, desperate to get us into their taxis or to stay at their resorts.

Laura and Flash, seasoned travelers that they were, got off and quickly ducked, weaved and sidestepped through the crowd like they were playing rugby for New Zealand. Dan was still ill, and, as a result, looked uncoordinated and walked stiffly. He and Kimmy followed me as I pushed through the crowd, smiling, nodding, and saying, "No, thank you. No, thank you," over and over again.

We eventually found Laura and Flash negotiating with a taxi driver in the car park. "Hurry up, you lot," said Flash. "Jump in the back, this guy's taking us to Haad Yao." He pointed at the back of a Toyota Hilux. It had been converted into a makeshift bus; they'd put two bench seats in the back tray with a cover.

"That looks about as comfortable as that fucking bus we were just on," said Dan.

"Harden up, you pussy, it's fine," I said in jest.

However, Dan had had enough of my teasing. "Listen, ass-hole, I've just spent ten hours, in a hundred-degree fucking toilet that belonged to Satan himself. Then, I was sick in the world's most foul-smelling and repulsive shitter that kept me vomiting longer than I should've been. So don't fucking tell me to harden up."

"Sorry, mate. I guess I've been putting the boot in while you're down, a bit too much today, eh?"

Dan's face softened, "Not really. I'm just feeling ill . . . I'm, you know."

"We'll be there soon, dude. Then we can relax, all right?"

"Sounds good."

We didn't have too far to travel from the ferry wharf: about 20 minutes, passing through a couple of little villages on the way. All the roads were filled with people, locals and tourists, riding scooters—it seemed like the preferred mode of trans-port on the island—and, like Bangkok, they were beeping their horns incessantly.

Haad Yao beach was beautiful. The sand was creamy white, with crystal-clear water quietly lapping at the shoreline. The kind of stuff you see plastered over the fridges of friends who have been on holiday to a tropical beach. You know, the friends, who, every time you looked at it for more than two seconds, give you an obnoxious ten-minute recount of where it was and how amazing it was. Those friends.

All along the beach were resorts, about ten of them. Laura and Flash led us south to a smaller place called Ibiza Bungalows where they had stayed before. It was basically a small restaurant that was surrounded by about 20 bungalows. The average bungalow cost about 500 baht, which was about 15 Australian. Dan wanted air-conditioning, so he ended up paying around double; the bus trip must have really scarred him.

Laura and Flash chose one closest to the water, and I grabbed the one next to theirs. Kimmy hadn't made a decision and just stood quietly beside me. I turned to her and asked, "You okay, Kimmy? What do you want to do?"

"Is it okay if I stay with you? Like we did back in Bangkok? I'd feel safer that way," she quietly whispered.

"Yeah, of course. I told you I'd look after you, and I think I'd sleep easier knowing that you're right there next to me."

"Hey, Kimstar, you can come and share with me if you like. I've got air-conditioning," said Dan, interrupting my moment of gallantry.

"Um . . . I'm okay. Thank you, though."

Inside our bungalow was a double bed with a fan on the ceiling. It had a small bathroom, which had a sink, a small shower that sprayed cold water only, and a toilet. It was a Western type of toilet, but it didn't flush. Instead, there was a large bucket of water with a bowl floating in it. Once you had done your business, you scooped the water into the toilet with the bowl. Hanging next to the toilet was a garden hose you used to spray your backside if you took a poo—it had quite the pressure too, like a water-blaster, and it hurt if you weren't too careful.

Flash told us a funny story about using them when he first came to Thailand. He said, "I'd been snorkeling in a bay when a bout of the old Thai belly hit me. So, I hightailed it up the beach, holding my butt checks firmly closed to stop the diarrhea from exploding down my legs.

"I ran to a beach bar and asked for directions to the closest toilet. It was about 20 meters away, but I made it just in time.

It was a traditional Thai toilet, which is basically a hole in the ground with a couple of small grooves either side for your feet. You have to squat over the hole and do your business." Flash squatted down, giving us a demonstration.

"When I got there, I just whipped my pants off and unloaded in a gush. I was in such a hurry I didn't notice there wasn't any paper, but just a garden hose with a pistol grip. I gave it a squeeze and discovered it had quite the recoil on it, with probably enough pressure to not only clean my balloon knot but take a few layers of skin off, too." Flash again gave us a demonstration as to how much it had recoiled in his hand.

"I mean, I wasn't sure whether this was for cleaning the shit off my ass or the wall, but it was all I had. So, I sort of maneuvered it around and came in from behind, trying to point it at what I considered the sweet spot. I closed my eyes, said a prayer, and gave the gun a squeeze. Unfortunately, I was about five degrees off and hit my ball sack instead. It fucking whipped it right up almost to my belly button. It felt like I'd water-blasted my balls right off. The funny thing was, the water shot right out the top gap of the door . . . I hope no one was walking by at that moment."

As well as ball-blasting hoses, the bungalows had little balconies with a table and chairs for two. We hung our hammocks across a couple of trees in front of Laura and Flash's bungalow. Dan tried to tie his dodgy string hammock between two trees as well, but the trees were way too close together. "Dude, there's no way that will go there. It's too small a gap," I said, watching him.

However, Dan completely ignored me and wrapped a quarter of it around each tree, leaving only half of a hammock to lie on— it was barely big enough to get his ass and torso in. Dan attempted to get into it, but he shook around uncontrollably like a newborn giraffe trying to walk for the very first time. Everyone in the whole resort stopped whatever they were doing and watched, wondering if he'd make it or not. He did. Wordless, he steadied himself, calmly lit a cigarette and stared out toward the beach like it was perfectly normal and perfectly comfortable. I thought he looked like a fat lady's leg in fishnet stockings: His skin bulged through the gaps in the string and, when he got off, he had diamond shapes imprinted all over his back.

The first thing we wanted to do was take a well-deserved dip in the sea and freshen up. We all got into the water, except Dan, who was finishing a cigarette.

"I can't believe we've been here less than 48 hours, and Dan has been drugged, raped, robbed, pierced and seasick," said Flash. "Generally speaking, any one of those things on a holiday is a major incident, but somehow Dan has managed to pull them all off in less than two days."

"Is he always like this, Myles?" asked Kimmy.

"Um, not really. I think it's because he's out of his habitat. You know, like a fish out of water. If we were in Sydney, he'd be, be . . . exactly the same. Actually, yes, he's always like this."

"Talking about water, how hot is it?" said Flash.

"Yeah, and really salty, too. It's going to sting Dan's nose when he gets in," said Laura.

"It'll probably be good for it," added Kimmy.

Dan finally finished his cigarette, and we all coerced him to get into the water. As he walked over the beach, we could see he was still a bit rough from all the unfortunate things that had happened to him. He must have been walking barefoot for the first time in his life, too, because he awkwardly tiptoed over the sand. It looked like he was walking on hot coals.

"How you feeling, mate?" asked Flash.

"Yeah, good, dude. The air conditioning in my room is awes . . . *Fuck!*" At that very moment, Dan stepped on something. "Jesus Christ, what the fuck was that?"

"Holy shit, dude, are you kidding?" said Flash, as we all burst out laughing.

"What was it?" asked Kimmy.

Dan quickly tiptoed into the water. "A fucking shell. It even drew blood."

"How the fuck did you cut yourself on a shell? There are only ten of them on this whole beach," I said.

Dan ducked underneath, and straight back up he came clutching his nose. "Fuck this!" he cried and got straight back out. He hobbled up the beach and sat in the shade, where he lit a cigarette.

"I told you," giggled Laura.

"I bet you he never swims again," I said.

We swam for an hour or so before rejoining him. When we sat down, he said, "So, I finally managed to get my phone to work and rang my parents."

"What did they say about your rape?" I asked.

"The old man just said, 'Way to be a fuckwit traveler.' My Mum was a little more concerned, but not as concerned as she was about my nose ring."

"Doesn't she approve?" asked Flash.

"Nah, she said if I don't take it out before I get back, she's going to get her labia pierced and show if off to all my friends."

"*What?* She didn't really say that, did she?" said Kimmy.

"Yeah, she did," said Dan, nodding.

"Are you going to take it out then?" asked Laura.

"Fuck, no. She's not serious. Look, they were just glad I'm okay."

"We've still got two weeks to go, Dan. Something tells me

you're not going to be okay," I said.

"I'll be fine, pimple-dick. Seriously, we're on a beach. What else could possibly go wrong?" he said smiling.

For the remainder of the day, we all kicked back with a few cold beers—each of us taking turns to fetch them from the resort fridge. When it was Dan's turn, he came back with a Sang Som bucket.

"Jesus, Dan, you don't learn, do you?" I said.

"What?" he said, with a mischievous grin.

"You're addicted to them, aren't you?

"It's the perfect drink. It's big, sweet and delicious, and it fucks you up. I think all drinks should come in a bucket with a straw."

As the day turned into night, we started to notice the effects of being out in the sun all day. "Did you get burnt today, Dan?" asked Laura.

"Yeah, Dan, you're really red," added Kimmy.

"Fuck! Thanks, Myles," he said, looking down at his burnt chest and belly that was so hot, there was a slight heat wave emitting from it. "Lie in the middle of the boat; it'll stop you from being sick."

"I didn't tell you to get burnt, you idiot. I was trying to stop you from throwing up. Besides, it worked, didn't it?"

"You know, this is the exact reason why I don't go to the beach. I'm not fucking built for it. Gingers and sun don't mix."

"Which is ironic, really, considering you're both orange."

"You know what's funny, Dan, is that you're only red on the front part of your body. Your back is still pale white. In fact, there's a perfect line from red to white running down your side," said Flash.

Dan couldn't help, but laugh with us. "Yeah, it feels real

fucking funny," he giggled.

"You'll be right, bro; it'll tan in a couple of days," I said.

"I don't tan, Myles. I'm like a crab. I turn red, and then shed my fucking exoskeleton back to white. See these freckles?" Dan pointed at his freckled arms. "That's my skin's piss-weak attempt at forming pigment."

"I just thought that's the complexion that gingers are born with. Some people are white, some people are black, and gingers have little brown polka dots, you know, like a Dalmatian."

"You're red, too, you know, Myles."

"Yeah, but I'll tan in a couple of days."

"Come on, let's eat," interrupted Laura, with a sigh. I sensed she was getting a little tired of Dan and me continuously giving each other shit.

All the resorts had set up little stalls at the water's edge selling fresh seafood caught that day. We strolled past and bartered for their produce and, once we settled on a price, they took our fish into the adjoining resort and cooked it to our liking. I ate two fresh oysters and a whole snapper for less than five dollars Australian—you can't even get a beer for that anymore.

It was a fairly quiet dinner because we were all beat from traveling and laughing. "You know, it feels like we've already been on holiday for weeks because of all the shit that's happened to you, Dan," said Laura.

"I know, I was thinking the exact same thing. It's only been a few days, and I don't think I've ever laughed as much as this in my whole entire life," said Kimmy.

"Well, I'm glad you bastards are enjoying yourselves at my expense," he said grinning.

"Yeah, laughing at your expense, Dan, sure does take it out of you," I said, and put my hand on his shoulder.

Dan tried to glower at me but he just cracked up laughing;

we all did.

"Mate, I can't wait to see what happens to you tomorrow," added Flash.

"Yeah, well I think I'm done with entertaining you lot with my misfortune—tomorrow will be different," he said, wiping a tear from his cheek.

After dinner, we managed one last beer back at our resort before turning in.

As Kimmy and I lay on the bed next to each other, we shared a smile before drifting off to sleep—a strange dynamic, considering we didn't really know one another.

Advanced-Damage Shampoo

aura and Flash were the first to awake the following morning—they always were. Laura was on her balcony when I finally emerged to give Kimmy some privacy to dress. Dan's sunburn had taken a turn for the worse; it was starting to blister and must have been really hurting him.

Kimmy joined me on the balcony in time to watch Dan stiffly shuffle over to Laura. "Hey, Laus, have you got any sunscreen or moisturizing cream I could borrow?" he asked. "My sunburn is killing me."

"Sure, here you go." Laura threw him a bottle.

Dan juggled it before dropping it on the ground. He groaned as he bent down to pick it up. "Nice catch, big fella," I yelled.

Dan flipped me the bird.

He opened the bottle, squeezed nearly half of it into his hands, and started rubbing it all over himself: his face, torso, legs, and arms. "Hey, Flash, can you get my back?" he asked, as Flash arrived back from a dip in the sea.

"Sure, mate." Flash grabbed the bottle and started to rub copious amounts of it into Dan's back.

Laura disappeared into her bungalow and, just as Flash had finished rubbing the last of the stuff into Dan's back, ran back out holding an identical bottle. "Hold on, Dan! That's not sunscreen."

"What?"

"Sorry, I couldn't read the bottle without my contacts in."

"What the fuck is it, then?"

"Um . . . oh shit," said Flash, reading the bottle.

"What the fuck do you mean, 'oh shit?' What is it?"

"Advanced-damage shampoo."

"Advanced what?

We started gut-laughing hysterically. "Shampoo," said Flash again.

"Are you fucking serious?" he asked, and grabbed the bottle to confirm it.

"Yeah, sorry. The bottles are identical," said Laura.

"Okay, then," he stammered, as he looked down at his glistening torso. "Well, I guess I'll just go and wash it off then."

We were still pissing ourselves laughing as he slowly walked back to his bungalow for another shower. "Holy shit, that was funny. How much of that stuff did he put on?" I asked.

"Like, half the fucking bottle," laughed Flash, as he held the bottle up to the sunlight to see.

Kimmy was in hysterics. "Look," she cried, pointing toward Dan's bungalow.

White foam was spewing out of the drain directly outside his bungalow just like a giant snake firework, reaching nearly four feet.

It must've been forty-five minutes before he returned. "Did you get it all off?" asked Kimmy.

"As soon as I hit the water, I went up like a fucking Alka-Seltzer. It was like I was having my own personal foam party in there."

That got us all laughing again. "It took me six showers to get it off. What the fuck, Laura?" he grinned, good enough to see the funny side.

"Sorry. Like I said, I can't see without my contacts. Besides, the writing on that bottle is so tiny, and most of it's in Thai."

"Hey, at least you'll be clean, Dude," said Flash.

"Clean as fuck. I don't need to shower for a month."

The day was quite overcast but still really hot and humid. We spent most of the morning lazing around, either reading, lying in hammocks, swimming or, in Dan's case, smoking.

At around 11:00 a.m. Flash decided it was a good time to hit the booze. "Anyone keen to head to the bar?"

"It's still morning, babe, why don't you enjoy the beach?" said Laura, almost disgusted.

"Laura, the beach will always be there, but the bar could burn down any minute, and then we'd be left wishing we had gone to the bar."

"You can't argue with that, Laura," I said, and got up to join him. "You coming, Dan?"

"It would be rude not to, my friend."

"Kimmy?"

"Sure."

"Laura? Laura? Going once, going twi . . . "

"Okay, okay, fine. This is bloody peer pressure, though."

"It's beer pressure, babe," said Flash.

Groaning at Flash's pun, we walked up the beach to a resort

bar, choosing one that had a huge deck area with large tables big enough for the five of us. As we entered the table area, Dan hit his head on a lampshade hanging above us. It was made of a lot of small and spiky stakes of wood. *"Fuck!* What was that?" he said, rubbing his head. He inspected the lampshade above him. "Who makes a lampshade out of needles and then hangs it right where people stand?"

"Only you could find that lampshade with your head, Dan. You could very well be the unluckiest man alive," said Flash.

Dan hit that thing a total of three times during our beers and lunch. By the third time, I thought he was putting it on, and said, "Dan, seriously, it's right above you. You can't be that stupid."

"Yeah, Myles, I love getting stabbed in the head by needles."

"Well, you did get your nose pierced with a needle," said Flash.

"True, you did get a needle stabbed directly into your nose and, if I recall correctly, you loved it," I added.

"Look, fuck-knuckles, I'm not stabbing myself in the head on purpose, all right? I think that last time actually drew blood." Dan inspected his hand after rubbing the wound.

"How the fuck did you even make it to adulthood, Dan?" I laughed.

"It's like this," said Flash. "If you placed a hundred baskets with lids all in a row and hid a snake in only one of them, and then asked Dan to randomly pick one by putting his hand in it, I bet you a million bucks he'd choose the one with the snake."

"Yeah, but if you were to put a million dollars in one of those baskets instead of a snake, Dan would never find it," I laughed.

"Exactly," agreed Flash.

"You're both hilarious," said Dan, still rubbing his head.

After lunch, we went back to our resort. There was a table in the sand near our bungalows that we had made our permanent spot. It had a large flax canopy that sheltered us, in particular Dan, from the sun. We sat around there a lot, drinking beers and chatting.

The people who worked the resort were so relaxed about the drinks. All we had to do to get a beer was walk into the open resort, help ourselves to the fridge, write down what we took on a blank piece of paper, and then stab it on a metal spike. It was an honesty situation, like farmers might do outside their farms, selling fruit or vegetables.

"They're so trusting, these Thais, eh? How do they know whether we're putting the right number down or not?" said Dan.

"Because they're only a dollar,' said Flash. "You'd have to be the tightest prick on earth to rip them off a dollar."

"Good point, but we are drinking a shit load of them. That spike is going to be phonebook-thick by the time we're finished."

As nighttime approached, we went for a leisurely stroll to the very end of the beach where some of the bigger resorts were. We stumbled upon a corner store that also sold fireworks, and Dan found a massive skyrocket that came with a four-foot mounting stick. "Dude, we have to get this," he said, holding the rocket out to me with his eyes bulging with delight.

"Oh, my God, yes!" cried Kimmy.

It ended up being about 45 Australian, which made it the most expensive thing we'd bought since arriving in Thailand.

"What the hell is that?" said Laura when she saw it.

"This, Laus, is tonight's entertainment," replied Dan.

"I can see that flying straight into your bungalow and burning it to the ground knowing you."

"Never mind the bungalow; it'll burn the whole fucking resort to the ground if he's got anything to do with it," added Flash.

"Koh Phangan will actually cease to exist if Dan lets that thing off," I laughed.

"Whatever. This bad boy is going to blow your minds," said Dan.

"Yeah, literally."

We strolled back down to our part of the beach to eat dinner. Again we chose fresh fish from a little stall outside a resort and had them prepare it to our liking, which actually consisted of a long list of options that none of us could decipher.

"I could get used to this," I said, after parting with another five dollars for a huge fish cooked to whatever-the-guy-said perfection.

"Hey, listen. We've got an idea about what to do tomorrow. We should all hire scooters and take a ride to Haad Rin," said Laura.

"Scooters!" yelled Kimmy, thrusting her arms in the air, startling the rest of us. "Sorry, scooters! Yay!" Kimmy said, softly and only lifting her arms halfway up.

"What's Haad Rin?" I asked.

"It's where they hold the famous full-moon parties. It's much bigger than here, with more of a party atmosphere. We can check it out and see what you guys think," said Flash.

"If you end up liking it, we can stay there for a few nights, too," said Laura.

"Sounds like a plan. What do you think, Dan?" I asked, as Dan quickly and quietly devoured a whole snapper in record time.

"That sounds absolutely riveting," he replied sarcastically, and washed the last of the fish down with his beer. "Come on, let's fire this baby off." He held his skyrocket up in one hand, a cigarette lighter in the other, and on his face a grin from ear to ear that would've given the Cheshire Cat a run for his money.

"Oh, dear," said Laura, rolling her eyes.

We paid for dinner and walked back to our resort. Dan started burying the skyrocket stick in the ground. "Here, give me that, you crazy bastard," I said, grabbing the stick. "We weren't fucking joking before, you know."

I buried the skyrocket stick into the sand, making sure it was pointing toward the ocean, but as I rotated it to get it farther down, it partially snapped. "Whoa, whoa, whoa! What the fuck are you doing?" cried Dan.

"It's fine, dickhead, it just cracked a little bit. Here, put the rocket on." I stepped back and let Dan set up the rocket.

"Fuck this, I'm getting way back," said Laura.

"Hang on! Wait, I'm going to film it," giggled Kimmy, getting her camera ready.

"Ready?" asked Dan, as he struck the lighter.

"Yes!" We all yelled in unison.

Dan lit the fuse and ran back to where I was standing. The fuse spluttered and fizzed till it disappeared into the rocket. We waited with baited breath, and then, whoosh! It took off six feet into the air, and then straight down into the ocean. Not one bang, fizz or pop.

We all burst out laughing—except Dan, of course. He stood gobsmacked. "What the fuck!" he said and started laughing, finally seeing the funny side of it. "What just happened? You didn't put the stick in right."

"Yeah, yeah, it was the stick," I said through tears.

Kimmy was gut-laughing so much she was rolling in the sand.

"That was the worst firework in the history of fireworks,"

said Flash. "You could've lit a fart that would have been more of an explosion—at the very least more exciting."

"It was bloody Myles' fault," he giggled, walking back toward our camp.

"Dan, I think you need a beer, mate," said Flash, putting his arm around him.

"Thank you, Flash."

"At least you didn't burn the island down," giggled Laura, as we sat at our table. Kimmy couldn't talk because she was still laughing.

Once we finally turned in for the night, Kimmy and I brushed our teeth and slumped into bed. We giggled together about Dan's firework. "He was so excited, I wish it would have been better for him," she said, as we lay together, looking up at the ceiling.

"Yeah, he's had a hard time of it, eh?"

"Yeah, he deserves a break."

Minutes went by without either of us talking, and I thought Kimmy was asleep. It was boiling hot in our bungalow, and the fan wasn't helping. I turned to get comfortable. Our feet touched and she turned to face me.

Was she asleep? Did she do that on purpose? Did she want me to kiss her? These thoughts raced through my head at a million miles an hour. I slowly edged my face toward hers. I thought to myself, maybe she does, or maybe she doesn't? Either way, it'll just look like I'm getting comfortable. I was thinking too much. I can't sleep like this. But our lips touched, and I kissed her and she kissed me back.

I didn't really mean for that to happen, but it did and I liked it. We kissed passionately for a few minutes, probably more, before we fell asleep. It was perfect.

I awoke some time later in the early hours of the morning; maybe it was six o'clock. I couldn't think straight. What would Dan think, what would my sister think? She's much younger than I am. I'm supposed to be protecting her. But I wanted her. Kimmy stirred, and then turned to face me. We didn't say anything but just looked at each other; we kissed again. What would Dan think?

No Sarong

Early the next morning we all met for breakfast, which was always an anomaly, for me in particular. "What do Thais eat for breakfast?" I asked, perusing the incredibly large menu. There was bacon and eggs and that sort of thing, but that was there for tourists, and since I had suddenly decided I wasn't one, that I was an experienced traveler, a traveler who lived by, "When in Rome, do as the Romans do," I wanted a traditional Thai breakfast.

"I'm not really sure. I've seen some people eat a sort of soup before, but I'm not exactly sure what it is," replied Flash.

"Yeah, I think they eat a type of rice porridge. I forget the name," said Laura.

"Rice porridge? Why don't they just make it out of oats like the rest of the world? They'll be making rice steaks soon," said Dan.

"Well, I think I might start eating fried rice for breakfast, noodles for lunch, and then fish for dinner," I declared, chucking the menu on the table with a satisfied grin over my face. Except, when I ordered, the waiter gave me a rather puzzled, almost disgusted look, and my grin quickly disappeared off of my face and suddenly appeared on Dan's, along with a chuckle and a shake of his head.

After we ate, we inquired of the resort owners about hiring scooters for the day. They had a bunch there that we could use for a couple hundred baht. Laura and Flash got one between them, while the rest of us got one each. Dan and Kimmy hadn't ridden a scooter before, so we got them to take a spin around the car park to practice before hitting the road. Kimmy seemed to pick it up fairly quickly, a little rough at making a full turn, but otherwise okay. Dan, on the other hand, took to riding a scooter like he took to climbing into hammocks—shithouse. "Dan, relax a bit. It's just like riding a bike," I said.

"I don't ride bikes, dickhead, I drive cars," he said, wobbling around the car park.

"Oh, sorry, Michael Schumacher."

"You'll be all right, mate. Just stick close to me and take your time," said Flash.

The roads were windy and very steep at times. People rode scooters and drove the odd car without, it seemed, any road rules. All the horror stories I'd previously heard of tourists crashing and injuring themselves while riding scooters in Thailand made complete sense, and then I suddenly realized I hadn't checked any of my scooter's safety features—like indicators, lights or the emergency horn. Mind you, I was pretty certain that the locals used the horn for everything but emergencies, like greeting friends, gaining the attention of girls, or generally letting the rest of Thailand know you have a horn.

"How fast are we supposed to go?" I yelled at Flash, "I

haven't seen one fucking road sign."

"I have no idea, whatever feels safe, I guess."

Dan struggled at times to get up the hills, and he continuously lagged behind. "Come on, fatty!" I yelled one time, zipping past him.

"Fuck off, dick!" he yelled back, with a face of intense concentration.

Laura and Flash led us through a few little towns, which we navigated by pure instinct rather than road rules, and then finally the township of Haad Rin. It was a lot bigger and busier than Haad Yao, or any of the towns we'd just ridden through, for that matter, and it was filled with just as many travelers bustling through the streets as locals. It was as though someone had lifted Khao San Road and dropped it right there on that little island.

Desperate to cool off, we parked up and headed straight for the beach. As we reached the edge of the sand, we all stopped in our tracks and stared. It was stunning. The whitest sand I'd ever seen in my life, with crystal-clear, miniature waves softly breaking on the shore. "Wow" was all we could muster.

What ensued was a whirlwind of sand and clothes as we started running across the beach and into the sea. Even Dan dived in. "We're staying here from now on," I said, when I surfaced.

"Oh, my God, yes!" agreed Kimmy.

We swam till our fingers and toes were prunes, and then headed back to the beach. Our sarongs we spread out like towels over the piping-hot sand, so we could dry off and get a bit of sun before lunch. Everyone except Dan, that is. He just stood there soaking wet; his cotton shorts heavy and dripping in sand, right in front of me. "What's wrong?" I asked, knowing exactly what was wrong.

"I don't have a towel," he quietly mumbled.

"Sarong, Daniel, a sarong. You don't have a fucking sarong."

"All right, dickhead, I don't have a sarong."

"But you do have a ridiculously large lighter, a few useless bracelets, brand-new shoes, a lovely photo of an iguana on your shoulders, a pierced nose . . . oh, and those shorts that don't dry for hours, even in this weather."

"Yeah, dude, if you lay them all out on the sand, you could create yourself a nice little spot to sit on," added Flash.

"Move over and let me sit on your sarong, Myles."

"Piss off. I told you back in Bangkok to buy a sarong about ten times. And, if I remember correctly, you told me I had a vagina," I said smugly.

"I stand by that comment . . . " He mumbled something else, but I missed it because he had already started walking back to the edge of the beach where he found a step to sit on. I watched him pouting for a while before I tutted, picked up my sarong and relocated at his feet.

For lunch, we popped into a resort that had a restaurant right there on the beach.

"I don't know about you guys, but I really want to stay here. This place is fucking amazing," I said.

"Yeah, me too," said Kimmy.

"Just so you know, Mr. I'm-a-seasoned-traveler-fuck-the-tourist-bullshit, this is the most touristy place on the island," said Flash. "But . . . I've got no problem staying here for a few days."

"Well, we'll settle our bill at the other place, and get a taxi down here tomorrow morning," said Laura. "We might as well go and check out some places to stay while we're here."

Dan didn't contribute to the discussion; he was busy eating. "Dan, what the fuck are you eating?" I asked. He was shoveling some sort of weird dish that he'd chosen from the menu quietly into his mouth—duck, I think. He seemed to like ordering the things you'd expect to see on a menu at your local Chinese restaurant or the Western dishes like southern fried chicken or chicken schnitzel: the things that Thais make to please tourists but have no idea how to make, the very things I had decided I wasn't going to eat.

"What?" he said, with his mouth full, and a poised fork of food ready to replace whatever he was spitting in my face.

"Never mind. What do you think about staying here for a few nights?"

"It's beach," he spat, and then shoveled another fork full of food into his gob before adding, "It's the same as the other one. I really don't care, to be honest."

"So, I'll take that as a yes, then?"

Dan ignored me.

After lunch, we strolled down one end of the beach to look for accommodation, finding a humble resort that was set up in a similar fashion to our current place—bungalows on the beach with a bed, fan, bathroom and balcony. They had three in a row available.

"You cool without air-conditioning, Dan, if we get these three?" asked Laura.

"Yeah, I don't really care about that anymore. I was mucking around with it at the other place and I think I broke it. I freeze my nuts off every night now. I actually have to sleep with the door open to keep warm," he said laughing.

"Jesus Christ, Dan," said Flash, shaking his head and giggling. "Only you could manage to freeze in the hottest country on Earth."

Before heading back, we went for a little ride inland and

happened across some elephants on the side of the road that you could feed bananas for a couple of baht.

Dan hit the brakes so hard he nearly went over the handle-bars, and then disappeared into a little cloud of smoke that had been created from skidding the rear tire. Kimmy did the exact same thing, but shouted *"Elephants!"* at the top of her lungs. The rest of us had to hook U-turns.

Dan and Kimmy were already parked and holding bunches of bananas by the time we reached them. "Here you go, pal," said Dan, wearing a smile from ear to ear as he offered me a couple of his bananas.

"Thanks, mate. They're not quite tigers but at least they're exotic."

"Yeah, dude. Elephants will suffice."

"Don't you find it weird that there these two huge animals on a tiny island like this?" I said, letting the trunk of one of the elephants curl around a banana in my hand.

"Yeah, and I don't really like the fact they're chained to that tree," added Laura.

Kimmy and Dan ignored our comments. They were giggling like a couple of shy schoolboys seeing a pair of boobs for the first time in their lives. "It's sniffing me," squealed Dan, as the elephant started searching his body for more bananas.

"I'm not surprised. Aren't they the same shorts you've been wearing since we got here?" I said.

"And undies." laughed Flash.

Kimmy and Dan, in particular, had grown in confidence with riding the scooters, so we made it back to our resort in half the time it took to get there. We had a quick snooze, and then a few beers before heading out for dinner.

The resort we'd chosen that night to cook our fresh fish had a couple of young boys on as staff. I noticed when Dan went to the bathroom, he was approached by one of them. On his return, Dan whispered to me, "That kid just sold me some pot," and nodded toward the young waiter.

"No shit? I saw you talking to him, and was wondering what he wanted. How much was it?"

"Fifty baht. We had to do the deal in the toilet. It was pretty dodgy, and I'm not sure how good it is either."

"Nice work, bro," I said, patting him on the back.

After dinner, we gathered at our table in the sand and rolled a joint. I inhaled deeply, holding the smoke in my lungs till I felt the drug enter my body and relax me; it was nice for a change. I hadn't smoked marijuana for many years, and it didn't take long before I was completely stoned. It also didn't take long to make me feel quite paranoid, very sleepy, and wanting to go straight to bed, and then I suddenly remembered why I didn't smoke marijuana.

We all retired to our separate bungalows, all except Dan. He wanted to keep going and smoke more pot. He followed Kimmy and me back to our room like a stray puppy. "Dan, we're going to sleep," I said.

"Come on . . . one more joint then I'll go, I promise."

"Nah, I'm done, mate."

"Kimstar, what about you?"

"No, thanks, Dan. I'm fine."

Dan walked out onto our balcony and sat in one of the chairs as I closed the door. "What's he doing out there?" asked Kimmy.

"I think he's smoking pot on our balcony." I looked out of the window at Dan. He was making himself comfortable in one of our seats and puffing away on a joint.

"Why doesn't he go to his own balcony?"

"I have no idea why he does 99 percent of the things he does, Kimmy. I've just grown to accept it."

Kimmy and I lay down on our bed. We held each other close, kissed passionately, and made love for the very first time.

I lay on my back as Kimmy rested her head on my chest; her hair smelt of the sea and the overhead fan was making it tickle my neck. "We can't tell Dan about this. He'll be devastated," I whispered.

"I know, I won't."

We feel asleep.

You Can't Get Sick on Mushrooms

The following day we were so excited about going to Haad Rin, that we ate breakfast at almost the same pace as Dan. We settled our bills and organized a taxi to pick us up. As I untied my hammock, I noticed Dan's was still tied to the trees. "Dude, come and get your hammock."

"I can't get it off the fucking tree."

"Did you even try?"

"I can't be bothered. It's uncomfortable anyway."

"It's going to be left as a reminder for all those who come after us as to how not to hang a hammock," laughed Flash.

"I'm seriously going to come back in a couple of years, just to see if it's still there," I said.

"Oh, it'll be there, all right. Why would anyone bother to steal that piece of shit?"

Our taxi arrived, and we all piled into the back and headed to Haad Rin.

At our new resort, the manager held out three separate keys and explained to us that two had double beds and the remaining one had two singles. "That works out perfect, since you two are sharing," said Dan, grabbing one of the double bed keys.

Kimmy and I looked at each other, but we were obliged to take the singles; we didn't want to let on about what had been happening between us at night. "That kinda sucks," whispered Kimmy on the way to our room.

"It's okay—we'll just push them together."

"But what if Dan comes in and sees them together?"

"We'll just tell him we're sharing the fan."

"Oh, yeah, nice."

While I was setting up the beds and hammock, Kimmy's phone beeped. "Oh hey, I've got a couple of friends coming here later today. Would it be cool if they hang with us for a bit?"

"Of course. Who are they?"

"A guy I work with and his friend. They're a lot of fun; you'll love them."

We finished setting up and cracked a few beers on Dan's balcony, since it was in the middle. "This is more like it," I said, lying back in my chair and letting the sun kiss my face. "Even you must admit, Dan, this is fucking paradise?"

Except, Dan didn't answer. He just sat there, slowly sipping a beer and puffing on a cigarette while staring at a bar up on the peninsula.

"Dan?"

"Holy shit, that's the mushroom bar," he suddenly cried, pointing at the bar.

"The what?" I asked, as we all strained our eyes to where he was pointing.

"That bar up there—it sells magic mushroom shakes.

"How the fuck do you know that?"

"My flat-mate told me there's a special bar up on a peninsula that sells magic mushroom shakes. That has to be it, dude. We've got to do mushroom shakes."

"Fuck that, Dan. The last time I did mushrooms, I was probably 19, and I threw up everywhere."

"Yeah, I'm not so keen on magic mushrooms," added Laura.

"I've never tried them before," said Kimmy, "what are they like?"

"It's the most amazing thing you'll experience in your life, Kimstar. It's like traveling through the stars to another universe," informed Dan, the man who knows everything there is to know about drugs. "They're supposed to be awesome over here, really mellow and nice."

"Hmm . . . I'm not so sure. That sounds pretty full on."

"Seriously, Kimstar, they're awesome. You'll have so much fun, I promise. We have to go up there and ask for a special shake very discreetly because it's highly illegal over here."

"Well, I don't give a shit. I'm not doing them because they made me sick last time," I said.

"What the fuck are you talking about? You can't get sick on mushrooms," he said, laughing. "Look, you can't come all the way to Thailand and not do the mushrooms. It's like . . . It's like, going to a brewery and not drinking a beer," he exclaimed, starting to get red in the face. "My flat-mate said you can just do a half if you're feeling a little precious. Kimstar, you should probably do half."

"Dan, for the love of God. I'll do them with you if you'll just shut it," said Flash.

"Thank you, Flash."

Most of the day was spent lazing around; we read books, swam in the sea, and sunbathed while Flash drank beer and Dan smoked cigarettes.

Kimmy and I were sunbathing after a dip in the ocean when Dan approached us, "Hey, you want to head in the town for a bit?" he asked.

"What for?" I said, without moving.

"I need undies."

"Dan, you need a lot more than just undies—remember our sarong conversation yesterday?"

Dan sighed. "Look, do you want to come, or not?"

"Yeah, I want to get some stubby holders anyway." I held up a half-empty beer bottle before adding, "These cold beers last all of ten seconds in this heat. You want to come, Kimmy?"

"Sure," she replied, getting up.

We strolled the little cramped streets of Haad Rin, momentarily ducking into shops to take advantage of the air-conditioning. "You know, I've noticed a bit of a theme happening here," I said after we ducked into a shop that sold a lot of useless crap.

"What?" asked Dan.

"Every single shop here is the same: either a bar, an Internet cafe, a tattoo parlor, Thai massage, a pharmacy, a shop that sells stuff you don't need, or a restaurant, and then repeat. Seriously, we must have passed about 30 odd tattoo parlors, and we've only walked three blocks."

"Myles, what else do you need?" said Dan. "This place is perfect: booze, drugs, food, tattoos, massage, and trinkets. They're the staples of life."

"What are you talking about? The staples of your life, maybe."

We found a large store that sold almost everything you could think of. Dan went searching for underwear, while Kimmy and

I looked for the elusive stubby holders.

It seemed an impossibility, so I eventually asked a young Thai girl who worked there by means of a quick game of charades. She duly led us to the very back of the store and handed us a packet of six stubby holders—it was all they had in the whole store, maybe the island. Those stubby holders ended up being the hardest thing I had to find in Thailand. You can procure morphine over the counter in any one of the 25 pharmacies in Haad Rin, but when it comes to keeping your beer cool while drinking in 40-degree heat, it's virtually impossible to find anything—the one staple they overlooked.

When I got to the counter, I threw an emery board in with the coolers because my nails were getting too long. Dan shortly met us there, but empty-handed. "Where are your undies?" I asked.

"I couldn't find anything I liked. It was all crap."

"Learnt your lesson after the hammock affair, did you?"

"Yeah, something like that."

"If it's any consolation, Dan, Myles just bought a nail file," said Kimmy, with a sly grin on her face.

"Jesus Christ! You really don't have a penis at all do you?" he said grinning.

"My nails are getting too long, and I don't have anything to sort them out," I tried, but I knew very well Dan had me beat on this one.

"Did you know he brought a pint of aftershave with him? Only it was confiscated at the airport because it was too big, too fucking big, I tell you."

"Thanks for throwing me under the bus, Kimmy."

Kimmy shrugged her shoulders and laughed with Dan.

"Look, when are we going to do the fucking mushroom shakes?" said Dan, changing the subject.

"Seriously, Dan, I'm going to stab you in a minute," I said.

"What, with your nail file?" This time, I had to laugh too.

When we got back to our bungalows, Laura was reading, while Flash was drinking and already surrounded by a lot of empty bottles. "I think you're going to be pretty impressed with my shopping today, my friend," I said to him.

"Why, what did you get?"

"Voila!" I cried, pulling one of the beer coolers out of the bag.

"Fuck me dead; I've been looking everywhere for those."

"Tell me about it," I said, and threw him one.

"I've been drinking these things at pace, so they don't go warm on me."

"That's your excuse?" I said, motioning at all the bottles.

"Yeah, it's fucking hard work, I tell you.

"Hey, what's that guy doing out there?" said Kimmy, pointing at a guy out on the beach all by himself, sitting in the fetal position.

"I have no idea. I've been watching him for a while. He looks like he's giving birth, eh?"

We all watched him for a moment before he suddenly got up and started drawing a large circle in the sand with a stick.

"What the hell is he doing now?" said Laura.

"I bet you ten bucks he's tripping on mushrooms," said Dan.

"Yeah, and I'll bet he's drawing an imaginary fort," said Flash. "Nothing bad can get him in that circle."

"I think he's drawing a fucking landing pad for the aliens, dude."

"Either way, he's not exactly helping with the idea of doing magic mushrooms tonight," said Flash, probably starting to regret his decision to do mushrooms with Dan.

Once the guy finished his circle, he sat in the middle, again in the fetal position.

"How bizarre," said Laura.

As we continued to stare at the man in the circle, we were suddenly interrupted by the arrival of Kimmy's friends. "Oh, my God," screamed Kimmy, and wrapped her arms around one of them. "How are you? I can't believe you're here."

His name was Johnny; he was a young French-Canadian traveling with his friend Rodrigo, a Brazilian guy. "I'm good. So good to see you, too," he replied.

We all introduced ourselves, and they sat down to join us. The very first thing that Johnny said was, "So, are we going to do magic mushrooms tonight?"

"Oh, thank, Christ," sighed Dan. "You and I are going to get on just fine, Johnny. These guys have been moaning about it all day." He turned up his nose and started to talk like a little child and mimic me. "I don't want to do mushrooms because they make me sick."

"Are you serious? You can't come to Haad Rin and not do the mushrooms," said Johnny.

"Right! That's exactly what I've been saying," cried Dan.

"All right, all right. I'll try the mushrooms," said Kimmy, immediately giving in.

"Thank you, Kimmy. Flash is in. Myles, Laura?"

Dan gave Laura and me a stern look. "All right, I'll do half," said Laura.

"Okay, Daniel, just for you, I'm in," I sighed, completely weary of the whole ordeal.

"Oh, my God, I think I just came in my pants. Come on, let's go."

"Hang on. Maybe we should eat something first," said Laura.

"Yeah, we'll all go after dinner," added Flash.

An hour or so passed before we all walked up the beach to a restaurant for dinner. Dan set a new, personal-best that night and impatiently waited for the rest of us to finish. "Shall we go, then?" he kept saying the entire time we were eating.

"Settle the fuck down, Dan," I said, and made a point to eat slowly.

After dinner he walked ten steps ahead of us, urging us to hurry as he led us up a set of wonky steps to a bar aptly named Mountain Bar. All the way up there were huge signs proclaiming "Magic Shake at Mountain Bar" or "Special Shake at Mellow Mountain," with huge arrows pointing us in the right direction.

"Ask very discreetly, eh, Dan?" I yelled from the back.

However, Dan didn't hear because he was already at the bar ordering a shake. Kimmy and I shared one, as did Laura and Flash. The other three did one each.

"Remember what your flat-mate said, Dan," warned Kimmy.

"I know what I'm doing, Kimstar," he replied with a wink, as he drank his shake in one gulp.

Kimmy and I gradually sipped ours, and it actually tasted better than I expected. The mushrooms I tried as a kid tasted terrible, but this was mixed with enough fruit to hide the feces-like taste of raw psychedelic mushrooms.

"How long will these take to kick in, Dan?" asked Flash.

"Oh, about half an hour, I reckon."

Oh, great wise one. He who knows all about drugs, how wrong he was. Within ten minutes he suddenly leapt to his feet and started pacing back and forth, taking deep breaths.

"You all right, bro?" I asked.

"These are pretty full on, eh?"

"Really? Mine hasn't come on yet."

Dan started peeling off his T-shirt. "Fuck, it's hot. Are you guys hot?" he said, as he started mopping errant sweat from his brow.

"No, not really," replied Flash.

"Fuck, I think. I think . . . I might be fucked."

Mine started coming on slowly. "It's making all the colors brighter and more beautiful. Sounds are louder and sort of echoing a bit for me," I said, looking at my surroundings that had definitely started to change.

"Yeah, same, it's like . . . remember when you would highlight a passage in a book at school?" said Flash.

"Yeah."

"Mushrooms are that highlighter."

"What the hell are you talking about?" said Laura.

"And if you wave your hand really fast, a slight trail is left behind," added Kimmy.

Johnny giggled, "If you laugh, it echoes."

We all started giggling, and then giggled some more just about the fact that we were giggling. All except Dan—he paced up and down chain-smoking cigarettes. "Dan, sit the fuck down. You're making me nervous," I said.

"Can we go back down the beach?" he asked, "I suddenly feel the need to draw a circle in the sand."

"Holy shit!" laughed Flash. "That dude *was* tripping on mushies."

We all got up and made our way back down the wonky steps that, for some reason, didn't seem as wonky as they had on the way up. "I think whoever built these steps must have constructed them while tripping on mushrooms," said Flash.

We found the same circle that we had watched being drawn earlier. "You'll be safe in here, Dan," said Kimmy, giggling.

Flash stood watching the water lap at the sand for a while

before turning to Laura and saying, "Have you ever noticed how symmetrical water is?"

"Yeah, it's like all the bubbles are exactly in the right spot," she replied.

"How does it do that?" said Flash, putting an arm around her shoulders.

"It's simply amazing," she sighed.

No one else said a word. It was kind of magical and peaceful and nice just standing there watching the water roll in and out.

Feeling thirsty, we eventually left the circle to grab a beer. The first bar along the beach was playing reggae and had little tables that were illuminated with candles and surrounded by mats out on the sand. Dan collapsed onto the first mat he came to.

"This is a fucking oasis, for the state we're in," said Flash, dropping next to him.

"I know. The Thais have really set this place out perfect, eh? You start at one end of the beach by getting fucked up on mushrooms. Then, when you're tripping balls, you wander down here to relax with some reggae and beers," I said, finding a mat opposite the table to Dan, "and who knows what the fuck is going on down there, but it looks amazing." I pointed down the beach where we could make out a lot of fire and people dancing to loud dance music.

For the most part I was actually enjoying the mushrooms, and so, it would seem, was everyone else. Dan, on the other hand, was freaking the fuck out. He mostly laid on his back, wide-eyed and staring at the stars, but periodically he would jump up and pace a bit, scratch his head, smoke a cigarette or mutter to himself. Johnny and Rodrigo seemed to be doing okay, considering they too had taken a whole one each. Mostly they just laughed a lot, but they did come up with the idea of going to the half-moon party—a monthly rave held in the middle of a forest a wee way out of the town. The rest of us decided that a long taxi ride, a forest trek, deafening music and a mosh-pit sounded like the absolute last fucking thing that we'd like to do while tripping on magic mushrooms, so the boys duly left while the rest of us stuck it out on the beach.

We all started drinking beers again—except, of course, for Dan, who seemed content to quietly stare at the sky and contemplate his existence—if that's what he was doing.

"Where is all that noise coming from?" asked Laura.

"What noise? Do you mean the music?" I said.

"No. It sounds like there's a group of people chatting right behind us, but when I turn around there's no one there."

"Never mind that, these fucking elephants up in the stars keep trying to grab me with their trunks," said Flash, reaching into the sky as he lay on his back.

"Um, oh . . . kay. How are you doing, Kimmy?" I asked.

"I'm fine, no elephants or disappearing crowds. Maybe I should have taken a whole one, too."

"Seriously?" I pointed at Dan, who was still lying on his back with his mouth open and staring up into the sky.

"Yeah, maybe you're right."

Bob Marley's "Three Little Birds" came over the stereo. "This music reminds me of when I sat my High School Certificate," said Flash.

"Why?" I asked.

"Well, I'd been listening to Bob Marley's 'Legend' album nonstop at the time, and during my English exam I was asked to write a creative story, which stumped me a bit as I didn't have a fucking clue where to start. Anyway, I looked around for inspiration and panicked because everyone else had their heads down, writing hard. It was then that this song popped into my head, so I started to write the words. 'Rise up this morning, smiled with the rising sun. Three little birds, pitch by my doorstep. Singing sweet songs of melodies pure and good.' Obviously there was a little improvisation on my part near the end, just in case the teacher was a Bob Marley fan. In the end, I managed 83 percent for that exam, and now I can't help but smile every time I hear this song."

"So, you basically plagiarized Bob Marley to pass English?" I asked.

"Yes."

"Fucking legend, no pun intended."

As the effects of the mushrooms started to wear off a little, I got bored with sitting in the one place. "Shall we check out what's happening with all the fire down there?"

"What, Dan's crotch?" joked Flash.

"Speaking of Dan, where is he?" asked Laura.

We looked at his empty mat, and then looked around the beach, only to find him standing at the water's edge, staring at the bubbles the waves were making on the shoreline.

"Come on, Dan, we're heading up the beach for a gander," I yelled.

"Everything is so beautifully symmetrical and symmetrically beautiful," he replied, without moving.

"See!" What did I tell you!" yelled Flash.

I walked down and put my arm around his shoulders to lead him back up the beach toward the fire. "Come on, big fella. Let's go for a wee walk, shall we?"

As it turned out, the fire was a bar right in the middle of the beach called Cactus Bar. Loud dance music blasted out of numerous speakers, and around eight fire dancers twirled sticks and pois, which they constantly dipped in kerosene and relit—the place reeked of it. Travelers danced along with them while others watched.

We grabbed another beer each, except Dan, who seemed to be mesmerized by the flames.

"You sure you don't want a beer? It might make you feel better," I asked.

"I'm not in the mood for drinking," he mumbled without shifting his gaze.

"Or talking, or walking, or general coherence," I added.

Dan continued to ignore me.

We continued to explore down the beach. Along the back were little shacks, maybe fifty of them in a row, all selling buckets. They had extremely offensive signs painted on them, like: "King Kong Fuck Bucket," "Fucking Free Fuck Bucket," "Fuck You Long Time," or "Bethlehem's Bucket, Jesus' Favorite," just to name a few. The stall owners leaned out waving frantically and yelling profanities like, "Come get fuck bucket here," or "Free fucking kiss with bucket." It had me somewhat perplexed because they were all selling the exact same thing: there was not one point of difference, the buckets were all the same, a hip flask of Sang Som, a little bottle of Red Bull, and a can of Coke.

As we neared the end of the beach, Flash found a basketball hoop stuck in the sand with little markers leading away from it. The farther back you stood to shoot the basket, the better the prize would be should you make the shot. The prizes ranged from Sang Som buckets to bottles of vodka. The game had finished for the night, but that didn't deter Flash trying his luck. Dan was uncharacteristically quiet as we all watched Flash try and try again. Even when I got up to have a go, he didn't say a word. I lined up from the farthest point and shot the ball. Bang! Straight through the hoop on my first go.

"That's what I'm talking about," I yelled, not moving my hand after I threw it, like I was throwing a three-pointer in the

NBA. Flash shook his head.

"Did everyone see that?" I asked, returning to Laura, Kimmy, and Dan with my arm still in the air, but they didn't reply. "Guys? Did you see that?"

"Yes we saw, smart ass," replied Laura.

"I actually got it on camera," said Kimmy.

"Sweet! Dan, did you see that?" However, Dan continued to play the mute and just stared at the ground. "Dan? Are you okay, mate?" I said, walking over and putting an arm around his shoulders.

"I probably should've had half," he finally said, without looking up.

"Ya think?" I chuckled. Not because I thought I was right, but because I wanted Dan to find the funny side of it, too, to maybe snap him out of it. It didn't.

"Look, bro, I think the worst of it should be over now. You should come right soon. Mine has practically worn off."

"Yeah, I hope so," he said quietly.

Flash had finished playing with the basketball and rejoined us with a bucket, and said, "Let's head back to the fire bar."

Dan lagged behind as we all walked back down the beach. I stopped and waited for him to catch up.

"I'm fucked, mate. I'm going to bed," he said, as soon as he reached me.

"What, already? It's so early; we're just warming up."

"I'm not feeling the best, eh. I might just lie down for a bit and come back out later if I feel better."

"All right, brother, we should be around this bar if you do, okay?"

Dan slowly dawdled back to his bungalow, while the rest of us found a table at the Cactus Bar and settled in to watch the fire dancers.

A young Thai boy of about 15 had a Connect Four game hanging around his neck; he was walking around challenging people for a match over money. Flash couldn't help himself and agreed. Game after game they played, but the kid was too good. I thought it was pure genius on the boy's part. There were hawkers walking around the beach trying to sell trinkets and other crap much the same as Bangkok and, of course, there were the rows of screaming bucket stands. However, this kid had a brilliant idea. Instead of getting into the same racket as every other Tom, Dick, or Harry, he decided to master the shit out of a simple board game and gamble against drunk or high tourists. I quietly contemplated letting him know about the lack of stubby holders there in Thailand and the potential fortune he'd make walking around selling them.

"Babe, let it go, you're never going to win," said Laura, after Flash's ninth game.

Flash did as he was told, paid the young boy his money, and sent him on his way.

"How much did you lose?"

"A couple of hundred baht," he replied.

"You probably shouldn't be gambling while on magic mushrooms, dude," I said.

"I think you're right there, big fella, but once you start playing that fucking game, you can't stop, mushrooms or not."

"I think the kid's a fucking genius. He's made more money off you in ten minutes than any of these other Muppets walking around trying to sell shit."

As the wee hours approached, Laura decided it was time to turn in. She had to retrieve Flash, who was dancing on a table with an empty Sang Som bucket on his head. "You're out of control, babe," she laughed, dragging him by the arm. "Let's go back. I'm tired."

"Are you guys coming?" he said, as they passed Kimmy and me.

"Yeah, we'll be a few more minutes; we're just going to finish our beers," I said.

They disappeared into the night while Kimmy and I finished up. It was nice to have a moment alone outside of the bedroom to hang out together and not hide our affection for one another. We held hands as we walked home along the water's edge, letting the sea lap at our feet.

All of a sudden, we were startled by Flash; he was running down the beach stark-bollocks-naked with his penis flapping about.

"We're going streaking!" he screamed, and ran straight into the water. Laura was leaning over the bungalow balcony with both hands covering her face.

Kimmy and I couldn't stop laughing all the way to our bungalow. I thought to myself, I guess Dan was right: You can't go to Thailand and not do the magic mushrooms.

Where Are Your Jandals?

The next morning, we were all feeling pretty rough. Even the painkillers didn't help. Dan didn't even awake till the afternoon. When he did finally emerge from his bungalow, he looked like death warmed up, and probably the worst I'd seen him to date. "Fuck, bro, are you okay?" I asked, genuinely concerned.

"Dude, when I was walking back last night, I felt that something had gone horribly awry. My stomach started making horrible noises and I had to shit . . . badly. So, I ran back to the bungalow literally clutching my ass because my sphincter had given up working. I made the toilet just in time and proceeded to shit water for about three fucking hours."

"Oh, my God," said Kimmy.

"Yep, that's exactly what I was crying through the sobs and tears, Kimstar. Then later on, I got up to get some water because I was so fucking dehydrated. But, I'm barely out the door before I went off like a fucking sprinkler, projectile vomiting in all directions."

"Oh, my God," repeated Kimmy.

"I thought you said that you can't spew on mushrooms?" said Flash.

"It must have been the food I ate last night."

"You're kidding me, right, bro? You mean to tell me, that after eating Thai food for breakfast, lunch and dinner over the last week, you get food poisoning the very day you take mushrooms?" I asked.

"Well, yeah. What else could it have been?"

"So, it wasn't the mushrooms. It was your meal. Out of the seven meals that were served last night at the same restaurant, you got the dodgy one?"

"Yeah."

"Unbelievable, Daniel. Un-fucking-believable."

"How do you feel now, still sick?" asked Laura.

"Still rough, but I've stopped spewing and shitting."

"Well, if you had food poisoning you'd still be spewing and shitting, trust me."

"Did you drink any water from the tap?" asked Flash.

"No, not that I know of."

"Mate, it's got to be mushrooms, then,"

"Well, whatever it was, it multiplied in my stomach because I drank fuck all last night, and it was if I was basically skin holding liquid shit and spew.

The rest of the day was spent lounging around swimming, sunbathing, and eating. Dan couldn't manage the direct sun, so he stayed in his bungalow for most of the day, emerging only to get water or smoke.

So far, Kimmy and I had kept our relationship secret,

mainly because of Dan. However, as time went on, we stopped caring as much and got a bit sloppy. Because, sometime in the afternoon we were both lying in a hammock between two trees right in front of Dan's bungalow. Dan suddenly appeared on his balcony for a cigarette. As he lit up, he leaned over the side to see us in the hammock together. "What's going on here, then?" he said, surprising us in the process.

"Um . . . just chilling. What the fuck have you been doing all day, playing with yourself?" I replied, desperately trying to change the subject.

Kimmy whispered in my ear, "Shit! He has no idea, does he?"

"No, I don't think so."

I looked up at Dan; he was staring at us intently while taking long hard drags of his cigarette. You could just about see his brain processing what he was witnessing.

"You two fucks have hooked up, haven't you?" he finally blurted out.

We both burst out laughing. "No," I said.

However, Dan was not impressed. "Yes, you have, I can tell. You promised me you wouldn't hook up with her, Myles. What the fuck?"

"It just happened," I started to try and explain. "We're sleeping next to each other; what'd you expect?"

"Now I'm on holiday with two fucking couples. This is bullshit." Dan flicked his cigarette and went back into his bungalow.

"Fuck, he's pretty upset, eh? I said to Kimmy. "I better go talk to him."

I couldn't blame him for being pissed off because he was right. I had promised him, and, to make matters worse, I was almost certain he had a thing for her. "Mate, you really that pissed off?" I said, as I entered his bungalow.

"Well, yeah. Remember our conversation back in Sydney?

"Nothing has changed. If we hadn't told you, you wouldn't have ever known."

"Whatever, I had my suspicions last night when you two were sitting next to each other on the table. You were playing footsies."

"What? No, we weren't. For fuck's sake, Dan, you were tripping balls last night. You probably saw a lot of shit that didn't happen."

Dan sighed. "Look, I just didn't want to be on this trip with two couples, that's why I wanted you to promise."

"I know, I know, bro. I truly am sorry about that, but it just happened. We were sleeping in the same bed. I . . . well . . . she's hot, and . . . it just happened. And, mate, we've been feeling guilty this whole time. That's why we didn't say anything."

"Really? That does make me feel a little better." Dan offered me a smile. "I might go elsewhere on my own for a bit. Maybe try and meet some other people."

"Don't be stupid, bro, there's no point in being here without you."

Dan sat there for a while quietly thinking it over. "True. You'd get bored without my misfortunes to keep you entertained."

I cracked up laughing. "Yeah, dude. That's exactly right."

Dan laughed with me. "Okay. Well, I'm going to town for some more water and shit. I'll be back soon. Do you want anything?"

"Nah, I'm all right. I'll see you in a bit . . . hey, big fella?"

"What?"

"Shall we hug it out?"

"Fuck off, dickhead."

"I am sorry, mate."

"I know."

"I love you."

"Myles, I like girls, for fuck's sake."

Dan walked off into town while Kimmy joined me on Dan's balcony. "Is he okay?" she asked.

"He's fine."

Laura and Flash joined us not long after with beers in hand. I was still too rough from the night before to drink just yet, but Flash didn't seem to have a problem with it. "Myles, my friend, you just have to push through the first few, and by about four or five, everything's back to normal."

"Where's Dan?" asked Laura.

"He's upset, so he's gone into town for a bit on his own," I said.

"Upset? What about?" she pressed.

"Um . . . about Kimmy and me hooking up." I offered her a nervous grin.

"I told you, babe," said Laura, turning to Flash and smiling.

"Damn it," said Flash, and clenched his teeth in wry amusement.

"I bet Flash the other night that you two had got together. I could tell," she said, patting Flash on the back.

"Really? I thought we'd been pretty discreet," said Kimmy.

"Yeah, it wasn't until Dan saw us lying in the hammock together that he worked it out. How did you?" I added.

"I just knew."

"Well, I had no idea," said Flash.

"That's because you've been drunk 24/7," said Laura sarcastically.

The sun was starting to set by the time Dan returned. "Look," he said, and pointed to his feet.

"I can't believe my eyes!" I said.

There on Dan's cut and bruised feet were a pair of brand-new green and yellow jandals. "What made you change your mind?" asked Kimmy.

"I wanted to."

"Really?" I asked.

"Well, to be honest, when I went into town, the concrete was so fucking hot, it actually burnt my feet, so I bought a pair. I had to just to get back."

"Good on you, mate," said Flash, "they suit you too."

"Really?"

"Yeah, Dan, they look great. Why do you call them 'jandals' by the way?" said Kimmy.

"I don't, that's a weird Kiwi word."

"It's short for Japanese sandals," I explained. "A Kiwi had seen a wooden version in Japan on his return home after World War II, and subsequently made them out of rubber when he got back to New Zealand. I think he may have actually invented them."

"Here we go," said Flash, rolling his eyes.

"Japanese sandals, huh? I guess that makes sense. I know Australians call them thongs. In America, that's a . . ."

"G-string." I said.

"Yeah."

"Look, it's because the shape the rubber makes between your toes is called a thong, it's also why a G-string is called a thong too," said Flash, staunchly defending his Australian heritage.

That night for dinner, we walked to the other end of Haad Rin and found a pizza joint. Everyone decided it would be a nice change from Thai food—everyone except me. As far as I was concerned, I was practically a local now, and I didn't want to eat this Western—or 'farang' as the Thais say—bullshit my that stomach might not agree with. But, my vote counted for nothing against the rest of them, and as much as my face and bottom lip pretended to dislike the farang bullshit, my taste buds and stomach enjoyed it.

After dinner we slowly made our way back to the beach for one more nightcap before bed. We chose a bar in the middle of the beach that had mats and tables in the same fashion as the reggae bar from the previous night.

That's where Johnny and Rodrigo found us. "Hey, there you are. What are you guys up to tonight?" asked Johnny, as they sat down to join us.

"I don't know," said Kimmy, "probably an early night."

"Yeah, we're thinking of doing the same thing. We're still pretty tired from last night's party."

"Oh, yeah, how was that?"

"Well, it was hot and loud, and Rodrigo lost his underwear at some point, and then proceeded to ask everyone if they new where they were."

"Really?" said Kimmy.

"Oh, and he thought there was a frog in his shoe."

"There *was* a frog in my shoe!" said Rodrigo.

"Ask Dan what he lost." I said.

"What?" they both asked.

"It's a long story, but about 20 liters of water from every orifice," said Dan.

"Oh, my God," said Johnny.

"Bloody dodgy Thai food," said Dan, looking at me with a smirk.

I sighed, "Jesus Christ, Daniel."

Laura and Flash finished their beers. "Well, I don't know about you lot, but we're turning in. We'll see you guys in the morning," said Laura.

"Yeah, see you guys," added Flash, as they both got up and traipsed back to their bungalow.

Johnny and Rodrigo had just ordered a beer each, so the rest of us stayed to keep them company. The Cactus Bar was blaring its dance music, and it was hard to ignore. "What's going on over there?" asked Johnny.

"They have a bunch of fire dancers who put on games with the tourists. It's pretty full-on; we were there last night," said Kimmy.

"Oh, let's check it out."

We got up to join the party at the Cactus Bar, and that's when I noticed Dan wasn't with us. "Where the fuck is Dan?" I asked.

"He's over there," said Kimmy, and pointed toward the bucket stalls.

Dan was already walking back, sipping on a bucket. "What are the fuck are you doing?" I asked when he reached us.

"I'm sick of beer."

"I'm not sure drinking a whole hip flask of rum is the greatest alternative to drinking a little bottle of beer, and weren't you sick just hours ago?"

"Jesus Christ, it's like I'm drinking with my grandmother."

"All right, well . . . " I tutted and sighed. " . . . I'll give you a hand with it, then," I said, trying my very best to sound like I was doing him a favor, but in all honesty, I was struggling with beer too and felt like a change.

"Piss off, dude, what about that lecture you just gave me?"

"All right sorry. Can I please have a sip of your bucket?"

"Meh, meh, meh, whole hip flash of rum," said Dan like a five-year-old as he let me sip through the straws but held onto the bucket the whole time.

I had to admit, that with every sip we took, the better we felt. "Get another one, dude," said Dan with a grin, when it was finished, and pushed the empty bucket into my chest.

I made a beeline to a bucket stall, trying to block out the cacophony of swear words, sexual innuendoes, and sentences of broken English that were hurled in my direction from the different stall owners. I wasn't interested in finding a cheaper price or bartering, or talking in general, for that matter. *"Sang Som!"* I yelled to a guy behind the stall, using my best tunnel vision to block out his competition.

"Co?" he yelled back.

"What? Do you mean Coke?"

"Yah!"

"Yes! How much?"

"Fo you, two hundret!"

By the time I got back, Johnny and Rodrigo had started dancing on one of the tables and had attracted a bunch of girls. "Hey, check it out," said Kimmy, pointing to the girls gyrating against Johnny and Rodrigo. "Those girls think they're in with a chance."

Two of them even high-fived each other, but, unfortunately for the girls, both Johnny and Rodrigo are gay. "Oh, dear God, this is going to end in tears," I laughed.

"Looks like I better save them," said Dan, jumping on the table and stealing my bucket on the way.

"Come on," said Kimmy, following in Dan's footsteps.

"Here we go," I mumbled to myself and followed Kimmy up.

We all danced together on the table and drank bucket after bucket. The night wore on, and at some stage, the fire dancers started a game of limbo with the limbo stick drenched in flames.

Dan and Rodrigo joined the crowd to play, but the

numerous buckets didn't help their cause. Neither of them could get under it, and they both kept falling over in the sand in hysterics.

"Oh, my God, look at that!" cried Kimmy, and pointed at a young guy in the crowd. He was sitting on a bench with a Thai prostitute between his legs. He had one hand on each of her breasts like it was the most normal thing in the world.

"I guess if you're okay with hiring a hooker in front of everyone, then you're okay with molesting her in front of everyone," I said, shrugging my shoulders.

It was then that I stopped and took a moment to observe my surroundings. Most of the people were very drunk—us included—and a lot of prostitutes had moved into the fray; I guess drunken travelers are easy picking, as Dan had only just proved the week prior.

Kimmy and I finally sat down at the bar next to the table we'd been dancing on. Johnny and Rodrigo had both disappeared somewhere, but Dan was still up there dancing away on his own. A prostitute waved him down to talk to him. He nodded, and when he turned away he was laughing.

"Did she offer you sex?" I yelled.

"No, she told me to pull my pants up," he said, still giggling.

Kimmy and I couldn't help but laugh, too.

As we entered the wee hours of the morning, I could hardly keep my eyes open. "You want to head back, Kimmy?" I asked.

"Yeah, I'm beat, and it's starting to get a bit cagey now."

We retrieved our jandals from under the table Dan was still dancing on. "Dan, where are your jandals?" I asked, interrupting his dancing.

"Down there next to yours," he said, and bent down to look.

"Ah, no they aren't," I said smiling.

"Fuck! Someone's nicked them!" Dan stood up and scanned the many feet at the party in a futile attempt to spy the culprit.

Kimmy and I started gut-laughing. "For fuck's sake, Dan, you really *are* the unluckiest man alive, aren't you?" I said.

"I only just bought the fucking things," he said laughing, seeing the funny side of it.

"I know, dude. Flash is going to piss himself when he hears about this."

Dan shrugged and continued to dance by himself on the table, sipping what was probably his fifth bucket of the night. "Come on, twinkle-toes, we're going to head back," I said, waving him off the table.

"You know what, dude? You're a pretty shit dancer, eh? You've got to relax, you know," he said with a cheeky grin.

"Is that right? And you've got all the moves, have you?"

"Hell, yeah."

Dan started dancing from one side of the table to the other. It looked more like he'd stepped in dog shit and he was trying to wipe it off his feet than dancing.

"A-fucking-mazing, Daniel. I can see what you mean now," I said in my sarcastic best and shook my head with disbelief.

"Kimstar, who's the better dancer—me or Myles?"

"You're both just as good as each other."

"If I'm only as good as he is then I'm seriously shit," I laughed. "I'll never fucking dance again."

Before I could tell Dan it was time to leave again, he reached down and grabbed a prostitute who was leaning against the table. He pulled her up next to him to ask her to dance. She obliged without saying a word.

"Oh, my God," said Kimmy.

"Here we go again," I sighed. "Hey, Michael Jackson! We're heading back. Come on, let's go."

Nevertheless, like the nights before, he ignored me and kept on dancing with the girl. "Seriously, Dan, let's go. Remember what happened last time we left you on your own?"

"Nah, I'll be fine. Go on without me."

"Come on, Dan," tried Kimmy.

"Dan, could you, just this once, listen to us? I pleaded.

But he wouldn't budge, so Kimmy and I reluctantly left. "This is like déjà-vu," I said to Kimmy as we walked back to our bungalow.

"I wonder if he'll take that hooker home with him?"

"I doubt it, the Bank of Myles is heading to bed."

Three Pumps and a Place to Stay

I've always found it fascinating that certain things can influence what might happen in our dreams. It might be the morning sun shining into your eyes that makes it difficult to see, or the music from an alarm clock that you may dance to. In this instance, it was an incessant banging that crept into my subconscious that morning. A banging that did nothing more than annoy me both in my dream and when I awoke. "What the fuck?" I mumbled, as Kimmy and I stirred awake. "Who is it?" I yelled.

"Dan."

"What the fuck do you want?"

"I want you to open the goddamn door."

When I unbolted the door, Dan stood outside leaning on the door frame. He was a sickly shade of gray with bags under his eyes bigger than what he was traveling with. "What the fuck do you want?"

"Um, have you got 2,000 baht?" he whispered.

"What for, and why are you whispering?

"Um, to pay a hooker."

"What? Did you fuck a hooker?"

"What?" yelled Kimmy. "Did he bang that hooker?"

"Dan winced like he was in pain, "Shush, she's right behind me.

I peeked over his shoulder. A Thai girl wearing a tight blue dress was standing on Dan's balcony, looking in our direction. "Shit, sorry bro. So, what happened, you sly old fox, did you fuck her?" I whispered, giggling.

"Um . . . not exactly. I'll explain in a second. Have you got the money or not?"

"Hang on," I went back into our bungalow and grabbed everything I had. "I've only got about 1,900, will that do?"

Dan turned to the girl on his balcony and asked, "Is 1,900 okay?"

She nodded, and Dan snatched the cash from my hand. When he handed her the money, I heard him ask, "So, would you like to grab some breakfast?"

The girl gave him a funny look, as if to say, "Are you fucking mental?" and without a word, she quickly walked down the steps of the balcony and disappeared toward town.

"Jesus Christ, he just asked her to breakfast," I said, turning to Kimmy.

"What?" she cried, and got out of bed to join me at the door.

"What the fuck happened?" I asked, when he returned.

Dan laughed, rubbed the back of his head and sheepishly looked at me before quickly looking away. "Look, all I remember is dancing on the tables and then waking up in my bed. I totally blacked out again. I don't remember meeting her, let alone soliciting her for sex. You know I'd never do that." He paused to light a cigarette.

"When I did wake up, I was relieved that I was in my own bed and not in the same situation as last time. Then all of a sudden, like déjà-fucking-vu, that hooker walked out from my bathroom and said, 'Helloooo'," Dan said, in his terrible Thai accent. "I thought, fuck! Not again."

Kimmy and I burst out laughing. "What, just like before? You have got to be fucking kidding me." I said.

"I wish I was," said Dan.

"So, you *did* sleep with a prostitute?" asked Kimmy.

"I asked her, 'Did we had sex?' and she said to me, 'No, no. You too drunk, I have to carry you home. You maybe have three pumps, then fall asleep'."

"Wow! And you don't remember any of this?" asked Kimmy.

"Nothing. I asked her if we used protection, and she pointed to the floor. There were condoms strewn everywhere, but still in their packets. She said, 'No,' and pointed again, but this time at my cock. I looked down, and I still had a fucking condom on."

"No, way!" yelled Kimmy.

"Yeah, so you know? I . . . I didn't want to waste it."

"What the fuck do you mean?" I asked, immediately wishing I hadn't.

"Well, I started to jerk off, you know? To try and get my money's worth since she was still there."

"What?" screamed Kimmy.

"Holy shit, dude, that's fucked up!" I said.

"Dan, did you sleep with her or not?"

"No, she just said, 'Stop playing with yourself. You look silly.' Pretty uptight for a hooker, eh?"

"Dan, just when I think it can't get any worse or funnier,

you go and top it," I said.

"I know, right? She waited all this time for me to wake up so she could get paid. Three pumps and a place to stay, she should have paid *me!*" he said, so matter-of-factly I started pissing myself laughing again.

"And she didn't even want to have breakfast with you," said Kimmy, barely able to keep the smirk off her face.

"You heard that, did you?" he asked, and looked sheepish again.

"Yeah, not one of your finer moments, bro," I said. "Anyway, let us shower, and we'll go and get breakfast with you."

Dan smoked a cigarette on the balcony while Kimmy and I quickly showered. The three of us walked down the beach and stopped at a place next door to the Cactus Bar. Kimmy and I both ordered pad thai while Dan ordered a whisky and Coke. "What the fuck are you doing?" I asked. "Aren't you going to order food?"

"I'm not really that hungry," he replied, before turning to the waitress and asking, "Can you turn up the music?"

"Jesus Christ, Dan, it's 11:30 in the morning, what's wrong with you?"

"I'm still drunk," he calmly replied and lit a cigarette.

"Come to think of it, how were you going to buy that hooker breakfast, when you don't have any money?"

"Yeah, I didn't really think that far ahead. To be honest, I didn't actually want to have breakfast with her; it was a reflex action," he said with a smirk.

"Oh, I see. So . . . it's like an apology of sorts? Something you do when you wake up next to a girl and take her out for breakfast to say sorry for falling asleep on her, on just the third thrust of your little freckled penis?"

"Fuck off, it's to top up her energy from being fucked every

127

which way but Sunday."

"Why not Sunday?"

"That's when we have breakfast."

"You're an idiot," I said, and we all cracked up laughing.

Laura and Flash were relaxing on their balcony when we all returned after breakfast. "I need to go back to bed," said Dan, and he walked straight past them to his bungalow.

"What's wrong with the big fella?" asked Flash.

"You won't fucking believe what happened to him last night," I said.

"Myles, Dan could've been anally probed by aliens last night, and I'd believe you right now."

Between us, Kimmy and I told them about the Cactus Bar, the fire limbo, the stolen jandals, dancing with prostitutes, déjà-vu, and waking with up with a condom still on his penis.

"Are you serious?" said Laura, with a look of complete disbelief.

"Actually, I take back everything I just said. That is un-fucking-believable," said Flash. "When we left last night, everyone was ready for bed. What the fuck happened?"

"Dan bought a bucket—well actually, he bought several," said Kimmy.

"Oh, so Bucket Dan came out, did he?" said Flash, and clapped his hands in amusement.

"Yeah, he's still blind-drunk," I said. "He even asked the waitress at breakfast to turn up the music, and all he ordered was a whiskey and Coke."

"This trip is turning out to be the funniest fucking two weeks of my life. I don't think I ever want to travel without Dan again," said Flash.

"I know, it's getting out of control," said Kimmy.

"I'm starting to feel the opposite; I feel like I'm babysitting an invalid," I said.

"You're not babysitting him, Myles, you're just trying to. Best thing to do is embrace him for the crazy bastard he is, and just give him a little push back on the track every now and again when he derails a little too far," said Flash.

"I have no idea what any of that means," I said.

"Goddamn, I wish I had a video camera. He should be filmed. He's not an invalid at all; he's a fucking legend."

"I guess, you're right. I do have sore ribs from laughing."

That day Dan didn't emerge from his bungalow at all. The rest of us did exactly what we'd come to Thailand to do: We lounged around in hammocks, swam in the sea, bathed in the sun and sipped one-dollar beers.

Later that afternoon, Flash found Kimmy and me sunbathing on the beach. He handed me a cold beer, dropped down beside me, and said, "You know what today is, don't you, mate?"

"No, what?"

"The Super Fourteen semis."

"Oh, shit! I totally forgot. What time. Whose is first?"

"Yours. Crusaders play the Bulls and then mine, the mighty Warratahs play the Sharks."

"Sweet, where are we going to watch it?"

"That's the thing. It's Thailand, and they don't even *play* rugby, let alone watch it."

"Why the fuck did you tell me it was on then?"

"I didn't want to be pissed off about it on my own."

"Gee, thanks."

The three of us continued to sip our beers on the beach for another hour, in relative silence, until Laura eventually joined us on the beach, bringing with her another handful of ice-cold beers—she had been shopping in town. "You'll never guess what I've just discovered," she said with a huge grin as she sat down next to Flash.

"What?" we all said.

"Well, I was walking past a bar in town, and I overheard a South African guy asking the owner about the rugby. I stopped to eavesdrop, and guess what? They're going to put it on for him."

"Holy fucking shit, Laura. That's the second best news I've heard all day next to Dan and the hooker!" I said.

"What's this rugby about? You guys have been bitching about it all day," said Kimmy.

"Kimmy, you're in for a treat tonight. Not only do you get to watch the greatest sport ever invented, but you get to watch the greatest rugby team the world has ever seen."

"Yeah, the mighty Waratahs," said Flash.

"The Crusaders have won seven championships, and the Waratahs have won . . . ah . . . how many?"

"Let's have a beer to celebrate," said Flash, quickly changing the subject and reaching for the beers Laura had brought.

"I'll drink to that, my friend," I said, and we clinked our bottles together.

As we sat enjoying the moment, a gigantic cloud loomed in the distance. It looked more like a huge black alien spacecraft than a cloud as it slowly made its way toward the island, spitting bolts of lightning and rumbling with thunder. With it came a wall of water that crawled up the sand and eventually up to us; it was one of the most amazing things I'd ever seen.

We all ran for cover under our balconies as water teemed down around us. Then disaster struck. A huge bolt of lightning, followed by a loud clap of thunder, plunged the whole island into darkness. "Oh, my God, what just happened?" asked Kimmy.

"The lightning must've killed the power," replied Laura, "it happens a lot here."

A few lights came on one by one in some of the bars along the beach. "They must have backup generators," said Flash. "Pray our rugby bar does, too."

As quickly as it arrived, the storm passed overhead to reveal a clear sky at dusk. It was like turning off a shower; the rain went from torrential downpour to nothing. "Okay, let's get dinner and check to see if the bar is still open," I said. "I'll grab Dan."

I banged on Dan's bungalow door, "Dan, get the fuck up."

Dan appeared at the door wearing only underwear and looking much like he had in the morning. "What's going on?" he asked, rubbing his eyes.

"Get dressed, dude, we're getting dinner."

Dan slipped on a pair of shorts and locked his door. "Is that it?" I said.

"What?"

"All that you're wearing?"

"Myles, we're at a beach, for fuck's sake."

Once we were in town, we noticed that only a handful of the shops and bars had backup generators. "This doesn't look good," said Laura.

"Fuck! What shit luck." I said, when we stopped outside the rugby bar that was in complete darkness.

"I wonder if it's because Dan's with us?" said Flash, with a cheeky smirk.

"I guarantee you it's because Dan's with us." I said.

"Piss off, I hate rugby," said Dan. "If my luck had anything to do with it, the power would be on, because then I'd have to sit here with you two dicks getting all jacked up over men in tight shorts."

"It might come back on—the storm is over after all," said Laura, sounding more reassuring than I felt.

We walked farther into town to find a restaurant with a generator that could serve us dinner. Passing a little T-shirt shop on the way, Dan stopped in his tracks. "I need to buy a T-shirt, I've completely run out," he said.

"Dan, you should have run out on day two," I said, glaring at his naked torso.

"Yeah, and I want to buy one now."

"Hurry up. We'll wait for you out here."

We all watched from the street as Dan entered. "This should be a laugh," said Flash. "He can hardly walk properly."

"I know, and look how sweaty he is," said Laura.

Just one girl was working, and she followed him everywhere he went in the little shop, which, we could tell from where we were, made him nervous. Dan selected a T-shirt that had a print of a girl flipping the bird. He took it off the hanger and tried it on, and then turned to us for approval.

"Oh, my God. It absorbed all of his sweat," said Kimmy.

Sure enough, the once-pristine T-shirt was now covered in dark wet patches. We all burst out laughing. I guess he thought we didn't like it, because he took it off and tried to put it back on the hanger. Maybe it was because the shopkeeper was making him nervous, or he was still jaded from the night before, but for some reason he couldn't work it out and ended up wrapping it around the hook and just shoving it back on the rack. The poor girl had to fix it, while Dan moved on and selected another T-shirt from a different rack.

"He's trying on a V-neck number," I said, as Dan, this time, tried on a plain gray T-shirt. Again he turned to us for approval, but this time it was way too tight. So we only laughed harder. Dan put the T-shirt back in the same fashion as before, and once again the girl fixed it for him.

Dan did this another six times with various T-shirts, each time looking to us for approval. What with him sweating and bumbling around the shop, the poor girl following and fixing each shirt as he crudely bundled them over the hangers, we couldn't stop laughing, which only made him worse. In the end, he left empty-handed.

"Why the fuck didn't you buy one?" I asked, still laughing.

"Because you were all laughing at them."

"No, Dan, we were laughing at the way you hung them, and at that poor girl who had to keep fixing them up after you," said Laura.

"You probably should have bought the first one, since it's now soaked with your sweat," said Kimmy.

"That's exactly why I didn't buy it, Kimstar, it's dirty," he said grinning.

"You're fucking crazy, Dan. Come on, let's eat," said Flash, leading the way into town to find a restaurant.

We eventually found one that was still open from the storm and had the customary fish stall out front. The two girls went into the restaurant to find a seat, while Flash and I were left to select the fish. Dan wandered off on his own, to another clothing store opposite the restaurant, to find that elusive perfect T-shirt.

After ordering snapper, we met the girls inside. It had the distinct aroma of diesel fumes from the generator, and even though we couldn't see it, we could sure as hell hear it; we almost had to yell at each other.

Dan finally joined us wearing a plain brown singlet with orange piping. "Finally," I said, as he sat down. "How fucking hard was that?"

"You know I've got a keen fashion sense, Myles," he said,

without looking at me, and opened the menu.

"Dan, you have the fashion sense of a homeless bum."

"And this is coming from a guy who brought a ten-year's supply of cologne and a nail file to a beach island?" he said chuckling, daring me to continue.

I flipped him the bird in defeat, and then said, "Look, mate, I didn't order you anything from out front, because I didn't know what you wanted. We're all eating snapper. If you want that, I can go and order it for you."

"I'm not that hungry, to be honest. I think I'm going to take a leaf out of your book and have pad thai," he said, before fingering pad thai on the menu for the waitress.

"If only you'd have taken a leaf out of my book last night, and then you wouldn't have awakened next to a whore this morning."

"She was in my bathroom, actually."

"Oh, I'm sorry, the bathroom," I said, rolling my eyes. "Come to think of it, why are they always in the bathroom when you awake?"

"I have no idea, coincidence maybe."

"It's almost as though they'd rather wait on the toilet for you to wake up rather than lie in bed next to your double ass."

"Get fucked, Myles. Those three pumps were the best three pumps of her life."

"I'm sure they were, big fella. Due to the fact it was over after only three pumps and she still got paid," I said, grinning.

Dan's meal was promptly served well before our fish. He quietly shoveled it into his mouth and was finished within minutes. After lighting a cigarette, he took a long hard drag and stood up, "I'm going to go to bed for an hour or two. I'll meet up with you guys later."

"What? You've been sleeping all fucking day—I thought we

were going to watch the rugby?" I said.

"Myles, you know very well I hate sport. I couldn't give a flying fuck about your rugby," Dan made quote marks with his fingers on the word "rugby." "Besides, the power's out, so you won't be watching shit."

"Is there anything you do like, Daniel?" I asked.

"Right now, I like sleeping, Myles." And with that he was gone.

When our meals finally arrived, the snappers were so massive they could barely fit on the plate, "I can't eat all that, babe," said Laura to Flash.

"Yeah, it didn't really look as big as this when it was out front. We probably could have shared."

"No shit, Flash. You know I hate leaving food on my plate."

"Apparently it's considered rude if you eat all your dinner in China," I said, in an attempt to make her feel better. "It means they didn't feed you enough."

"This is Thailand, tool-bag. China is a long way over there," she retorted, waving her hand in the general direction of China.

"Babe, eat as much as you can. I reckon these guys finish off the leftovers anyway," said Flash. "So you'll be doing them a favor."

She rolled her eyes and started eating. When she finished, she put what was left on Flash's plate and said with a grin, "You can look like you didn't eat your dinner."

Flash tried to eat it but failed. "Just when you need Dan and his waste-disposal gut, he's gone and pissed off to bed," he said.

After our meals, we walked past the rugby bar in the hope it would be open. Sadly, it was still in total darkness. "Kickoff time is fast approaching, guys, and it isn't looking good, is it?" I said.

"Let's go and have a beer to drown our sorrows," said Flash.

"It doesn't matter what the situation is with you, does it? Celebration or gloom, there's always an excuse for beer," I said, as we headed down to the beach.

"It's not an excuse, Myles, it's customary . . . no, it's mandatory. It's the correct and moral thing to do. Think about it: If we didn't have a beer to celebrate things or to drown our sorrows, we'd be left high and dry, wondering what to do with ourselves in very intense situations, situations exactly like this. The world would be in a state of anarchy. It . . . it would be fucking pandemonium. Jesus, Myles, I need to have a beer just to calm myself down."

"Flash, none of that made any sense," said Laura.

"Beer makes the world go around, Laura. It's as simple as that."

We sat at a bar on the beach, one that had a generator, and ordered a few beers to, well, drown our sorrows.

"This is bullshit. I can't believe the power is out," I moaned. "It hasn't rained a single day since we've been here. Then a random, rogue cloud comes out of fucking nowhere for ten fucking minutes and ruins everything."

"I know, I think I would have rather not have known it was even going to be shown," sighed Flash.

"Well, kickoff is in ten minutes . . . no, nine minutes," I said, looking at my watch. "We're . . . "

Before I could finish, Kimmy yelled, "Look! The Mountain Bar just lit up."

She pointed toward the end of the beach, and she was right, it was—and so was the rest of Koh Phangan.

"You know what this means?" I said, as we all jumped up.

"It's rug-bee. It's rugby time," sang Flash, already making his way toward the bar.

"I can't believe it, with less than ten minutes to spare," I said, running to catch up to Flash.

Sure enough, when we got there, the bar was lit up with its television on. We all grabbed beers and positioned ourselves right under the screen, just as the coverage started.

They ran through the players of both teams, and before long, my team, the Canterbury Crusaders, started running down the tunnel toward the field.

I clinked my bottle of beer against Flash's and grinned. Then, without warning, the screen went black. A message on the television appeared saying we had to pay extra for rugby coverage.

"No!" Flash and I screamed in unison.

"What's going on?" I said to the lady behind the bar and waved frantically toward the television.

She tried changing channels but nothing happened. Flash and I offered to pay the extra money, but she was adamant that she had paid it and that it should be on. Nevertheless, it wasn't.

"No way, this is insane. What a day," I said.

"Maybe mine will still be on?" said an optimistic Flash.

"You're fucking dreaming, bro."

However, we waited anyway, drank beers and stared in bleak hope at the black screen. But just like my game before, it didn't come on.

"What a roller coaster of emotions," said Flash, "it wasn't on, then it was, then it wasn't, then it was and now it's not."

"I think I need something stronger than a beer to drown my sorrows now, dude," I said.

It was about 2:00 a.m. when we finally walked back to our bungalows. Flash and I walked like little kids who had been told we couldn't have any candy; we dawdled, stuck our bottom lips out, and kicked sand. We grunted good night at each other before going into our separate bungalows.

Just as Kimmy and I were drifting off to sleep, she was suddenly startled. "Oh, my God, Myles, there's someone out there on our balcony trying to look through our window."

"What the fuck?"

Sure enough, a silhouette was moving around trying to find a gap in the curtain to see in. He finally gave up and started banging on our door.

"Who is it?" I yelled.

"Dan."

I got up and opened the door to Dan standing in the doorway like the numerous times before, but this time he looked more confused than sick.

"What are you doing?" I asked.

"Are we going out or what, dude?"

"What the fuck are you talking about?"

"I thought we were going to watch the rugby or something?"

"First of all, you hate the rugby, and second of all, it's fucking 3:00 in the morning."

"Oh, I thought it was like ten or something. I've been walking around the beach and bars trying to find you guys. I don't have a watch, so I have no idea what time it is." He pointed to the empty space on his wrist where a watch would normally be. "Well, do you want to go out anyway?

"What?"

"I'm wide-awake now."

"Dan, it's because you've been asleep for over twenty-four hours."

"I know, so do you want to or not?"

"I've already been drinking all night, and I'm fucked. I'm sorry, mate."

Dan sighed, "I can't bloody sleep with all this fucking music either."

"Yeah, it's loud when you're not blind drunk, eh?"

"Fuck yeah."

"I'll see you in the morning, you Muppet."

"Night," he said, as I closed the door and returned to bed.

However, I couldn't get to sleep after that. Dan was right, the music was too loud and it didn't stop till six o'clock in the morning.

It's a Bag, Dude

Flash turned up at our bungalow at about 10:00 a.m. looking a few years older than he had the night before.

"I didn't sleep a fucking wink last night," he said. "It felt like I was sleeping in the middle of a dance party."

"I hear you, bro. Kimmy and I felt the same," I said.

"It was as though they'd put one CD on repeat all night. I kept hearing the same songs over and over again," said Kimmy.

"I may not know the names of any of those songs, but I now know the fucking words off by heart," I added.

"Look, Laura and I are going to move on. You guys can stay here if you like, but we can't take another night of that music."

"Where are you thinking?" I asked.

"There's a beach right at the top of the island called Bottle Beach. It's a lot more secluded than here, but it's fucking amazing."

"Can we still drink and party?"

"How many times do I have to keep telling you? It's Thailand; you can drink wherever the fuck you want. It's just quieter than this place."

"What do you reckon, Kimmy?"

"Sure, let's do it."

"Awesome. Get packing. Laura and I will go and get a boat sorted."

I knocked on Dan's door to let him know we we're leaving. "Bro, pack your shit, we're moving on."

"Where to?" he asked.

"To the top of the island. There's a beach up there that's supposed to be amazing, according to Flash."

"Oh, cool. Another beach. I can't wait," he said, sarcastically enough to piss me off.

"Well, where would you rather go?"

"I'm kidding. I do want to get back to Bangkok at some point though."

"Yeah, we will, dude,"

"I probably should have just stayed there this whole time," he said quietly, almost to himself.

"Dan, if you'd stayed in Bangkok, you'd be dead by now."

"Piss off."

"Really, dude? Do I have to remind you of the shit that has happened to you thus far?"

"Okay, you're probably right."

"Come on, mate. We'll have fun, I promise."

"Yeah, you say that a lot, mate, but all that ever happens is you having fun at my expense."

"Sorry. Come on, mate, so I can laugh at your expense," I laughed. Dan couldn't help but crack a smile.

Packed and ready to go, we all met at an Internet café to check the rugby scores, our emails, and to say farewell to

Johnny and Rodrigo.

"I need to buy a bag. I'll be back in a minute," said Dan, once they had left.

Flash and I were too engrossed on a sport site, reading the bad news to bother answering—both our teams had lost.

"Where's Dan? We've got to go," said Laura, ten minutes later.

"I think he said something about buying a bag," I answered.

"Oh, great!"

"Yeah, if it took him a week to find the perfect singlet, who knows how long it'll take him to find a bag. You guys go ahead. I'll wait for him here."

Dan took his sweet time, but he finally returned with a new bag. "What the fuck is that?" I asked, staring at something only a 12-year-old girl would own. About the size and shape of a bowling ball bag, and half the size of his other wee bag. It was made from shiny black vinyl, with bright, fluorescent pink corner accents, fluorescent pink piping and large, fluorescent pink Adidas logos either side.

"It's a bag, dude," he said, holding it up by its girly handles.

"You're taking the piss, right? This is a joke?"

"What's wrong with it? The lady said it suited me."

"It's pink!"

"What the fuck do you have against pink?"

"Dan, you never cease to amaze me. Just when I think I've got you figured out, you go and buy a little girl's bag. You won't buy a sarong to lie on because it's gay or buy jandals because they don't suit you. You spend nearly a week trying on and choosing one fucking singlet, yet you'll go and buy a pink handbag, the gayest fucking handbag in the universe."

"Whatever, it's just a bag," he replied, ignoring me.

"You're an enigma, Dan," I sighed.

We met with the others on the beach next to the boat they had hired. It was one of those long tail boats, which is basically a long, thin boat with a car engine at the stern—they use the drive shaft as a propeller.

"What the fuck is that, Dan?" asked Flash, pointing at his new bag.

"It's just a fucking bag. What's the big deal?" he shrugged.

"It's a fucking makeup purse, Daniel," I said.

"Look, it's all they had, and I needed a fucking bag to carry the rest of my shit around."

"What shit? You don't have anything," said Flash.

"Let's just get in the fucking boat already; it's just a fucking bag."

"It's a girl's bag."

"Fuck up, Myles."

The boat ride was quite the experience. It jetted along at a great but very noisy pace—the car engine didn't have a muffler on the exhaust. Every time we hit a wave, it jarred our asses and rattled our teeth, but we got to see the whole eastern side of the island from bottom to top, which was basically a lot of rocks and trees with the odd beach every now and then. We stopped off at one such beach called Haad Sadet for a coconut smoothie—my favorite Thai drink next to Singha beer—and a swim to cool off before continuing on.

As the boat rounded the top of the island, Bottle Beach came into view. It was more stunning than the last: brilliant white sand and crystal-clear water. I thought to myself, I can finally take a picture for my fridge and be that person who will say, every time someone looks at it for more than a second, "Ah, Bottle Beach. It's a beach on Koh Phangan, Thailand you know? I was there back in, I don't know . . . 2010, I think, probably the best beach I've ever been to." I will then sigh and let my eyes glaze over before adding something about how it changed my life and that I'm a different person for it.

As we got closer to the shore, I noticed that there were only four resorts on the entire beach—and, just as Flash had said, it was a lot more chilled than Haad Rin. I could count the number of people on the beach with one hand.

Our skipper cut the engine and drifted onto the beach. Of the few people on the beach, only one or two acknowledged our arrival, with a brief moment of stopping what they were doing, which was either reading a book or applying sunscreen, to watch us get out of the boat.

"Where to? I asked, as I waited on the beach for the rest to wade through the water holding their bags above their heads.

"Head to that one in the middle, Bottle Beach One," said Laura, pointing to the one directly in front of us.

"We've stayed there before; it's pretty good" added Flash.

"Well, what are the others like?" I asked, for some reason not convinced.

"It's got a pool . . . "

"Bottle Beach One it is," I replied, without letting him finish.

Like the other resorts we'd stayed in, the bungalows were the same. We couldn't get bungalows next to each other, but that didn't matter. The resort had a restaurant and bar right on the beach, and we knew that's where we'd be spending most of our time anyway. In fact, that's exactly where we headed after we each set up our bungalows.

"This place, is amazing, Laura," I said, taking a sip of my first beer of the day. "Leave the best till last, eh?"

"I know, we always finish here. It's perfect."

It was perfect: the sun was shining, music was playing, and

the beer was ice-cold.

"I think we might stay here till the end, eh?" I said to Kimmy, as I lay back in my seat breathing in the warm, salty air.

"I think so as . . . " she started to say, just as something fell out of a palm tree right into her lap. "What the . . . what the hell is that?" she screamed, jumping up and flicking her sarong.

Whatever it was, it flew toward Laura and landed in her lap. "What the fuck? It's moving!" cried Laura.

"What the fuck is it?" I asked, as Flash, Dan, and I jumped out of our seats, ungallantly keeping our distance.

Laura quickly flicked it off her lap and jumped to her feet too. Once it was on the ground, both girls started screaming, "It's a snake! It's a snake!

We all watched as a green snake slithered across the ground, up another tree, and disappeared into the flax roof above one of the other tables. The four guests sitting there suddenly dived out in all directions, as if a hand grenade had been thrown at them. A waiter ran over to investigate the kerfuffle.

"A snake just landed on my fucking lap," said Kimmy.

"And mine," added Laura.

"Wha kala?" said the waiter.

"Green, bright green!" said Kimmy.

"Ah, green snake . . . ah, not poison, no worry."

"Easy for you to say—it didn't land in your bloody lap," mumbled Laura.

After that, the waiter didn't let the girls live it down. When Laura and Kimmy ordered food for lunch, he said, "Pad thai wit green snake?" In fact, for the duration of our stay, he would ask, "You wan green snake?" every time the girls ordered any food.

This drove Laura insane in the end, so whenever she ordered anything, she'd say something like, "Chili basil chicken, please . . ." and as soon as the waiter was about to talk, she'd interrupt him with, *"No green snake!"*

After lunch and the snake ordeal, we took a dip in the pool, which, Dan reminded me, was a very fucking touristy thing to do.

"I think this could very well be the best beach I've ever been to," I said.

"Yeah, Flash and I love it here," said Laura, as she sat on the side of the pool, dangling her legs in the water. "It's also the best place to see plankton glow for some reason."

"What? Plankton glow?" said Kimmy.

"Yeah, like that sex scene in the movie *The Beach,*" said Flash. "When it's really late at night, disturb the water, and it will sparkle like stars."

"And the farther out you go, the better it gets," added Laura.

"Are you serious? We're trying that tonight," I said.

"Dan, do you like it here?" asked Kimmy, "Relaxing change from Haad Rin, huh?"

Dan was sitting at the side of the pool on a recliner. "Kimstar, it's a beach. It has salt water, sun, and sand," he said, and shrugged his shoulders.

"And cold beer," said Flash, holding up his beer bottle.

"It's its one saving grace."

"Should we check out that place up at the end of the beach for dinner?" interrupted Laura. "It's getting dark, and I'm getting hungry."

We all agreed.

After a quick shower, we ventured up to the very end of the beach to the resort Laura had suggested for dinner, which ended up being the best meal we'd had since arriving in Koh Phangan. "This place just keeps on getting better, doesn't it?" I said, when I finished my meal.

"Can you guys smell weed?" said Dan, sniffing the air around like a bloodhound.

"Yeah, this is a bit of a hippy resort. I think they might even let you smoke it here in the restaurant," explained Laura.

Dan's ears perked up, and he finally looked interested. "How do you get it?"

"I don't know, Dan. Ask the waiter," said Flash.

But he didn't; he just ordered his usual beer and Sang Som bucket.

"Dan, what are you going to do when you get home and you can't get buckets anymore?" I asked.

"I think I'm going to start an import business, specializing in Sang Som whisky and Red Bull syrup."

"That's actually not a bad idea, you know. Mind you, that much alcohol in a bucket would probably cost you thirty bucks in a bar."

"Exactly! We could get rich out of this, you know?"

"The only thing that you'd get out of it, would be cirrhosis of the liver."

As the night wore on, Dan started teasing me about being with Kimmy, but I was too tired for teasing. I got up and left the restaurant. Kimmy followed.

"Don't let it get to you, Myles, he's just venting," she said, joining me at the water's edge.

"I know, I don't blame him either. I'd probably be just as pissed off if it was him, and not me, you were with."

"But I'm not with him, though, am I? I'm with you," she said, and kissed me. "Come on, let's try this plankton thing Laura and Flash were talking about."

We waded into the sea up to our knees. I ran my hands through the water and, like magic, it started to sparkle. It was as though I was running my hands through the midnight sky disturbing the stars, and the harder I did it, the brighter they sparkled.

"Oh, my God. This has got to be the coolest thing I've ever seen," said Kimmy.

Suddenly, Laura and Flash waded past us. "You've got to get right in," said Laura. "It's much better farther out."

"You mean it gets better?" asked Kimmy.

"You better believe it." She grinned.

Kimmy and I took off our T-shirts and threw them back onto the shore to swim farther out, following Laura and Flash. "It's so warm," said Kimmy.

"I know, it's amazing," I said, slowly paddling out farther and farther. As our bodies glided through the water, the plankton glowed a bluish-white. I dived under and opened my eyes, and imagined I was flying through space. "It tickles," shrieked Kimmy, when I surfaced. "Can you feel it?"

"I can, beautiful. I can." I laughed with her as we embraced in the stars. "Everyone should experience this in their lifetime . . . even Dan." We kissed.

Very Powerful Man

I awoke the next day without a hangover for the first time since arriving in Thailand, and very hungry for some breakfast. Laura and Flash were already at the bar eating when Kimmy and I arrived. "Morning. Seen Dan yet?" I asked, as we sat down to join them.

"Nope, but I hope he's calmed down from last night," said Laura, "that got pretty awkward."

"Yeah, I don't know what to do about it," I said.

"He'll be 'right," said Flash. "He's just been having a bit of a rough time of it. I'm going to make it Dan Day today. Whatever he wants to do, I'll do . . . within reason, of course. I don't want to wake up in a foreign room with a stretched sphincter."

Our "green snake" waiter arrived to take our order, and I suddenly decided that my staunch "Only eat what they eat," rule had run its course, and that I needed bacon and eggs back in my life. "Full English, please," I said.

"Tea oh coffee?"

"Tea, please . . . English breakfast."

"Wha?"

"English breakfast."

"Yah, Engrish breakfah. Ah, baco' an' egg an' toas' come wit tea oh coffee?"

"Tea, please. I'll take the tea."

As we were eating breakfast, Dan finally emerged from his bungalow. "Morning," he said, sitting down.

"Morning," we all said, except Flash, who was grinning from ear to ear.

"You all right there, mate?" he said to Flash.

"How are you feeling?" Flash replied, slapping him on the shoulder.

"Not too bad this morning, actually." Dan breathed deeply while pushing his arms back and sticking his chest out.

"If you could do anything you wanted today, anything at all, what would it be?"

"Um . . . smoke weed and watch a movie," he replied, almost ignoring Flash and having a little moment to himself. He was probably imagining that he was sitting on his couch back in Sydney, smoking a bong while watching a B-grade horror flick. He liked that kind of movie because they were always full of naked women, as he once told me. I asked him why he didn't just watch porn? To which he replied, "You can't watch porn on the living room couch when you've got flatmates walking about, idiot." I told him that I thought there was something a lot more disturbing about someone getting turned on by horror films.

"How about we replace weed with beer and the movie with me?" asked Flash, interrupting his moment.

"Oh . . . kay," he said, like he was unsure of Flash's intentions.

After I'd finished eating, I got up from the table and said, "I'm going to take dip, and then lie on the sand for a bit."

Dan got up too.

"Where the fuck do you think you're going?" said Flash.

"I was going to . . . "

"Sit the fuck down, we're drinking."

Dan obliged and quickly sat back down. "Myles, aren't you going to drink too?" he asked, with fear in his eyes.

"Dan, it's 9:30 in the fucking morning. Are you mental?"

Laura, Kimmy and I left for a swim and a spot of sunbathing. "You know, I have a funny feeling it's Flash Day today, and Dan's doing whatever Flash wants to do," I said, when we were in the water.

"Oh, definitely," agreed Laura.

Laura, Kimmy and I sunbathed and read for a few hours before joining Flash and Dan again for lunch. Flash was pissing himself laughing. "You wouldn't believe what just happened," he said when we sat down.

Dan was shaking his head and giggling to himself. "Jesus Christ," he mumbled.

"What?" I asked.

"This is fucking funny. You know old Green Snake?" started Flash, pointing to our "green snake" waiter. "He came over here and said to Dan, 'You very powerful man.' He actually squeezed him on the shoulders when he said it." Flash paused to giggle to himself before continuing. "He asked him to help him move one of these massive tables."

Flash patted the table we were sitting on; it was a large log table that could easily sit four adults. "Dan's all chuffed, and he's puffing out his chest like he's Arnold fucking Schwarzenegger. They walked over there and grabbed an end each while I

151

sat here, waiting in anticipation for Dan to fuck it up some-how. But, fair play to the big fella, he seemed to carry the table okay, and he even put it down without any problems. Our waiter thanked him a thousand times, as they do, and Dan started strutting over here like a proud ginger peacock." Flash again paused to giggle.

"What?" said Kimmy impatiently.

"Out of nowhere, he stubs his toe on a piece of furniture and nearly rips his fucking toenail right off."

"He's taking the piss, right?" I said, glancing at Dan, who lifted his foot to display his bloody toe.

"I wish he was," he said. "It should probably hurt, but I'm so fucking sore all over I can't really feel it."

That was it. Despite Dan's toe, we all started laughing yet again. Even Dan laughed. "This is getting fucking ridiculous," he said, and buried his face in his hands.

"You really are the world's unluckiest man, aren't you? You should start your own brand. The man. The wound. The fra-grance . . . Infections from Dan, the unluckiest man alive," I said, in my best advertising voice.

"The man. The cock. The fragrance . . . Lost Inhibitions from Dan, the unluckiest man alive," chimed in Flash.

"Yeah, the ad would be a guy applying aftershave in the mirror . . ." I started.

"But, he gets most of it in his eyes, which stings and blinds him a little," added Flash.

"Yeah, yeah. Then cut to a bar, where multiple chicks swoon over him. Our guy smiles at camera and winks with red swollen eyes."

"And, when he leaves with one of them, he falls down the stairs because they're blurry."

"Cut to the guy waking up next to the chick who gets up

to take a piss. Only, she does it while standing." We all burst out laughing.

"Fuck off, you two," said Dan, but he too couldn't help but laugh.

"If I told this holiday as a story verbatim with every minute detail, I don't think anyone would ever believe it was true," I said. "I don't think anyone has ever been this unlucky in this short amount of time. I don't even think I've seen a movie that has as much shit go wrong for one person."

"I know. Mind you, it would make a pretty fucking funny movie, though," said Flash.

"Yeah, Matt Damon would be perfect to play the role of me," said Dan. "People reckon I look a lot like him."

"You're fucking delusional, Daniel," I said.

He just shrugged his shoulders and sipped his beer. "They do."

After lunch, we continued to do much of the same as we had that morning; Laura read on the beach, Kimmy and I slept in our hammocks, and Flash and Dan continued to drink at the same place they'd been since breakfast.

I awoke later that afternoon with a series of excruciating aches in my belly, like a series of Braxton Hicks contractions before a baby, and my God it felt like I was about to have a baby. I ran to the toilet and made it just in time to unleash wave after wave of hot putrid waste. I whimpered like a puppy as my body convulsed over and over again—it felt like I was vomiting, except it was coming out the other end. Once it was all over, I wiped the sweat from my brow, the tears from my cheeks, and then met the boys for a well-deserved beer.

"You wouldn't believe what just happened to me," I said, ordering a beer from Green Snake.

"Hang on . . . aren't I the one who's supposed to say that?" said Dan.

"What?" asked Flash.

"I was suddenly hit with the urge to shit, but I haven't been for a while. When I did, I filled the toilet with a gigantic mound of feces," I explained, making a mountainous shape with my hands. "It's the biggest shit I've ever done."

"Jesus, Myles, steady on," said Flash, wincing.

"I know, sorry. I've been popping painkillers for the hangovers, and they seemed to have backed me right up. It's the first shit I've done in three or four days, and when it finally came, it was like I was possessed by the devil."

"Okay, thanks, pal. Way too much information," said Dan, holding his hands out in front of me.

"I had to pour two of those buckets just to flush it."

"Really? I pour at least three or four of those when I go," said Flash, all of a sudden interested.

"No, not the little bucket, the fucking big bucket. The one the little bucket floats in."

"What, the drum?" asked Dan.

"Yeah!"

"Jesus Christ, dude, did it go down?" said Flash.

"Just. But it was touch-and-go there for a while. I had to start it off with the water blaster to loosen it all up, and then follow through with the drums of water. I thought I was going to flood the bungalow with water and shit."

We started laughing. "Okay, okay, we get it, you sick bastard," said Dan, through some tears. "I must say it's fucking nice to be laughing at someone else for a change."

"Well, we've all got a Thailand shit story now," said Flash.

"It's been a goal of mine, Flash, I have to admit," I said, jokingly.

"Welcome to the club, Myles."

"Welcome," said Dan, holding out his beer.

"Gee, thanks, guys."

The three of us continued to drink into the early evening. Dan was sick of beer at this stage and started to work his way through the cocktail list. "I'll have a mai tai, please," said Dan, to Green Snake.

"Beer?"

"Mai tai."

"Beer?"

"No, a mai tai," Dan asked again, slower this time and pointed at the menu.

"Mai tai for lady. Maybe not so powerful man," he said, laughing.

Flash and I burst out laughing. "Jesus, Dan, even Green Snake is giving you shit. I wouldn't let him see your makeup bag, if I were you," I chortled.

"It's just a goddamn bag," he said shrugging, but he couldn't help but laugh.

Soon after that, Laura and Kimmy joined us for dinner, and we continued drinking into the night. By this stage, Flash and Dan were completely off their faces. They were coming up to 12 hours of solid drinking, and the more Dan drank, the more belligerent he got.

Laura said she'd had enough and went to bed just as Dan started ordering Sang Som buckets. After he'd finished the first one, he actually started passing in and out of consciousness, right there at the table. "Dan, are you awake?" I asked.

"Yesh! Why?"

"It looks like you're sleeping."

"Flash. I mean, Morris . . . Myles, I'm not . . . I'm not sleeping, you fucking idiot."

"Okay, okay. Settle the fuck down."

"I'm . . . I got to pish," he slurred, and got up to walk to his bungalow. Bemused, we watched as he weaved between the palm trees and balconies, every now and then hitting one of them—it was hard to decipher in which direction he was trying to walk.

"Look how fucked he is," I said. "There's no way he'll be back."

"I know, I'll be surprised if even makes it into his bungalow," said Kimmy.

"I'll give him ten, and then check on him."

But I was wrong. Out of the dark, Dan slowly weaved his way back, hitting the odd palm tree and balcony on the way. He slumped back at the table and resumed drinking.

We managed one more beer before Kimmy and I retired to bed, leaving Dan and Flash to it.

The Wrath of God

Laura was eating breakfast alone when Kimmy and I awoke and joined her. "Where's Flash?" I asked, sitting down.

"He's still sleeping and bloody snoring."

"What time did he get in?" asked Kimmy.

"I have no idea, but it was probably the drunkest I've ever seen him."

"Yeah, they were still going when we went to bed at like 12:00," I said.

Kimmy and I ordered some breakfast and, when it arrived, so did Flash. "Mate, you look fucking awful," I said, as he slumped down next to Laura.

"And smell," added Laura.

"I feel worse," he stammered.

"What happened after we left?" asked Kimmy.

"Well, we kept on drinking. Dan must've drunk about three buckets in the end, and that's after drinking beer and cocktails

157

all day." Flash paused to drink a whole bottle of water in one gulp.

"Thirsty, babe?" said Laura, as sarcastically as she could.

Ignoring Laura, he continued, "So, we decided to go to the bar to try to mingle with the other guests. I told Dan I'd be his wingman, since he's alone. But when we stood up, he was so fucking drunk I literally had to carry him. And guess what, they actually cut him off from the bar." Flash tried to laugh but ended up in a coughing fit.

"I'm sure they did." I said.

"No one gets turned away from a bar in Thailand, Myles, no one. I reckon you could be wheeled up to any bar here, especially one as remote as this one, lying on a hospital gurney with an intravenous drip in your arm, and you'd still get served. But not Dan, oh no. He managed to write himself off so much, they actually turned him away."

"It could only happen to Dan," said Laura.

"It gets better," he said. "I tried to introduce him to some girls at one stage, but he couldn't even fucking speak; he just laughed in their faces. It actually freaked them out so much I had to apologize to them."

"Then what?" asked Kimmy.

"Well, we were somewhat castaways after that, so I ended up carrying him to his room and putting him to bed like a baby. Have you seen him yet?"

"No, but I'm fucking dying to see what state he's in," I said, with an evil grin.

Like on cue, Dan finally stumbled over to our table and, like the many mornings before, he looked terrible, even worse than Flash did. "How you feeling, big fella, okay?" asked Flash.

"Not at all actually," he said wincing. "What I'd do for air-conditioning right now. My room is like a fucking oven. It's making my head pulse like it's going to explode."

"I think that might have something to do with the thirty odd beers, numerous cocktails and three buckets that you drank last night," I said.

"Yeah, but if I was in air-conditioning, I'd be sleeping off the beers, cocktails and—how many buckets did I drink? I don't even remember drinking one."

"This is pretty much a regular occurrence for you, isn't it, Dan?" said Laura. "You've spent half your time on holiday with a hangover in bed and the other half blacked out."

"Yep, it's how holidays are meant to be spent, Laura. It's holidaying 101."

"Dear God," she sighed, and looked at the sky.

Dan ate some breakfast, much slower than usual, and then grabbed two large bottles of water and returned to his bungalow to try and sleep some more.

For most of the day, we did nothing more than swim, sunbathe, eat and, to the bewilderment of us all, Flash managed to start drinking beer again during lunch.

Later that afternoon, I spied Dan emerging from his bungalow; he fell into the chair on his balcony and straightaway lit a cigarette. I walked over to see how he was doing. "Hey, mate, how you feeling—any better?"

"You know, Myles, I've never wanted a girlfriend so much in all my life being here," he said, completely taking me off guard.

"Jesus, mate, what are you talking about?"

"This is the most romantic destination on earth, and I'm here with two couples."

"Come on, mate, it isn't like that. We're all here together, for fuck's sake."

Dan didn't say a word; he just puffed on his cigarette.

"Look, think about it. We're not lying on the beach cuddling and kissing, are we? Flash spends the majority of the day at the bar, remember? You spent the whole fucking day, and night, with him yesterday. You don't see Laura crying about it, do you?"

"I suppose," he sighed.

"Come on, bro, everyone is at the bar." I said, walking to our usual spot.

"Hey, big fella, how you feeling?" asked Flash, as soon as we arrived.

"Pretty average, but better than this morning, that's for sure," he said, flopping into a seat, but looking a lot less melancholy. "Hey, does anyone use those mosquito nets in their rooms?"

"No, why?" we all replied.

"Oh, it's just I opened the door to let the cool breeze into my room, only to wake up a few hours later with about a million fucking flies all over me. It was like that Irwin Allen movie, *Swarm*. It freaked me the fuck out, and now I can't get them all out. I'll have to try and sleep under that net tonight."

"Holy shit, dude, it's like the wrath of God with you, isn't it?" said Flash.

"Yeah! First cometh thy roofies and thou loss of all thy memories that thou had before," I said, in my best biblical voice. "Next cometh thy sickness, and thy stomach will empty by raging floods."

"For thy third, ye sun shall singe thou to blisters, and thy skin shall shed," added Flash. "And for thou fourth, a cut of thou foot that will bleed and sting in ye seas."

"And ye lure of ye succubus will be thou fifth. Stripping thee of all thou inhibitions and leaving thy testicles blue."

"And I will smite thee cunts, with great furious fucking anger, if thou don't shut the fuck up," said Dan, giggling.

We were all laughing together when we were startled by a loud shriek. We swung around and saw that it was the massage lady, jumping around inside her little beach bungalow where she gave massages to tourists. Next minute, she ran out of her bungalow with a thick piece of PVC piping and started whacking the ground with it.

The whole resort had now stopped whatever they were doing and were watching intently as she repeatedly hit the ground. When she finally stopped, she picked up what she was hitting and brought it over to the bar to show everyone. It turned out to be a huge gecko—the biggest I'd ever seen—it was about a foot long, a beautiful bluish color with orange spots.

"Gecko, gecko," she kept saying, as she held it up by the tail for all to see.

"No shit, did you need to kill it?" asked Laura, looking rather distraught. In fact, the whole resort was looking rather distraught. Nevertheless, the masseuse ignored her and continued to parade her kill like a proud cat that had killed a rat.

She walked over to a couple with a little boy of about five. "Gecko, gecko," she said to the boy, and held it up so he could see it. Suddenly, the gecko came back to life; she had only temporarily stunned it. The little boy gasped, and the masseuse shrieked, dropping it to the ground. Then again, she started to whack the poor gecko, right in front of the child.

"Jesus Christ, that kid's going to have nightmares from now on," I said.

"Nightmares? That kid's going to grow up to be a fucking serial killer," said Dan.

The masseuse finally picked up the now—dead and flattened gecko, took it down to the edge of the ocean, and threw it in. Unfortunately the waves kept washing it ashore, so she kept trying to throw it in deeper.

"Wow. Never mind the kid. I think I'll be having nightmares after that," said Kimmy.

A couple of hours and beers later, it was dinner time. We returned to the resort at the end of the beach that had the best food in Koh Phangan—according to me. As we were being seated, a huge electrical thunderstorm engulfed the island and started pouring rain. It was so loud we couldn't even hear ourselves talk—let alone each other. After dinner we all ran through the rain and went straight to bed, which I didn't mind at all—there's something wonderfully cathartic about making love during a thunderstorm.

Sunburn, Pooing and Buckets

For the first time in days, we all met at the exact same time for breakfast. "Hey, guys, can we head back to Bangkok tomorrow?" asked Dan. "I really want to do some shopping before we fly home."

"Of course, Dan," said Flash, putting his arm around his shoulder. "Anything for you, mate."

"I don't want to spoil anyone's holiday or anything?"

"Dude, don't be stupid, it's about time we headed back anyway," I said.

"I was being sarcastic."

"We'll sort everything out today so we can leave first thing in the morning," said Laura. "We should be able to get the train this time, so we can sleep properly."

"I can't believe we're actually going to leave," said Kimmy, almost in tears. "It's been so much fun, I don't want to go home."

"I know, back to reality," I sighed.

"For your last day here, Dan, I'm going to put a hammock on your balcony, and you're going to do something therapeutic if I have to put a fucking gun to your head," said Flash.

"What, like binge-drinking for 24 hours?" he replied.

"I don't know, read a book or write something. You're a fucking writer, aren't you?"

"Okay, okay. Fine I'll find something to do then."

After breakfast, Flash grabbed one of their spare hammocks and hung it for him on his balcony. While he was doing this, Dan went and bought a pen and a little notebook from a shop attached to the resort.

Kimmy and I watched him get into the hammock from our balcony that was four bungalows down. It took him a while, and it shook like crazy as he tried to slide himself into it. Nevertheless, he persevered, and he finally managed to get in and settle down. "He looks like a large sack of potatoes hanging from the roof, but at least he's getting the hang of it," I said.

"How long do you think he'll last?" said Kimmy.

"Ten minutes, max, knowing him."

However, Dan lasted more than ten minutes; he lasted all day. He only got up every now and again to eat, drink and urinate.

Sometime during afternoon, my nostrils were assaulted by the strong smell of marijuana coming from the bungalow next to ours—a young woman was lying in her hammock smoking a joint.

I whispered to Kimmy, "Hey, check out that chick next door. She's pretty cute, eh?"

"Yeah, I suppose. Why?" she said, after taking a sly peek at our neighbor.

"You'll see."

After a while, Dan got up to grab himself another beer,

passing us on the way. "Dan," I whispered, loud enough to grab his attention.

"What?" he asked, turning in his tracks.

"Ask that chick if she wants a beer," I whispered quieter, pointing to our neighbor.

"Why?"

"She's hot, she's alone and she's got weed," I whispered even more quietly, using universal sign language for large breasts and smoking a joint.

Dan surprised me: He boldly walked over to her and brazenly introduced himself. He said, "Hey, I'm Daniel. I'm staying down there a bit."

"Oh, hi," she replied, with an accent I was unfamiliar with.

"Um, I noticed you're all alone and, well . . . I'm about to grab a beer. You're more than welcome to join me, if you're bored, of course?"

"Sure, I'd love to," she replied, getting out of her hammock.

"Stay there, I'll get it."

Dan offered me a smile as he proudly strutted to the bar. I smiled back and dozed off to sleep in my hammock.

Laura and Flash were already at our spot drinking a beer when Kimmy and I joined them later that evening. Dan followed not long after. "Hey, how'd you go with our neighbor?" I asked, as he sat down.

"Okay. She's from Israel and traveling Thailand all on her own."

"What happened? Did you meet a chick?" asked Flash.

"Yeah, she's staying next to Myles and Kimstar. I asked her if she wanted a beer, so we sat and chatted for a while," he said proudly grinning.

"Nice work, big fella. Where is she now?"

"Well, she invited me back to her bungalow to smoke some weed, but I got so stoned I had to go back to my bungalow to lie down."

"Jesus Christ, Dan, you should have had her come to dinner or something," I said.

"It's all right I'll see her later."

That night after dinner, Laura invited a guy who was there on his own at the resort to join us at our table for beers. It turned out that he was from Christchurch, New Zealand like Laura and I. He was the same age as I, and, once we got talking, we found out we had mutual friends.

"So, Dan, how did your relaxing day in the hammock turn out?" asked Flash.

"Surprisingly good, actually. To be honest, it was probably the best day I've had since being here. You were right. I should have done that sooner."

"You're fucking shitting me?" I said.

"Shut it, Myles. What'd you end up doing?" asked Laura.

"Lay there pondering mainly, and I wrote three poems about my time here in Thailand."

"No shit? Let's hear them then," said Flash.

Dan pulled his little notebook from his pocket and cleared his throat.

"Sunburn," said Dan.
"The sun, it seems so happy, just chillin' in the sky,
but he's a sadistic bastard, and it's you he wants to fry.
Every waking moment he's plotting in his head.
More ways that he can catch you out,
and cook you like an egg.
You see, to him we look like steaks, and once our skin is bare,
it really makes him angry that we're all a bit too rare.

Nothing makes him happier than to burn you to a crisp,
sear you like a sausage, and fry you like a fish.
And when you lie there hurting, it's not enough for him.
He's coming up with other ways to peel off all your skin.
So, when you're playing on the beach, having just a ball,
just know the sun's a bastard, and he hates you most of all."

"Pooing"
"I'd really like to poo again, or maybe I could pass.
Thai bathroom facilities are far from world-class.
I know that once I poo again, and once the deed is done,
I'll have to spray my asshole with a fucking water gun.
I still need to poo again, but maybe it can wait,
before I spray the open eye of my tender rump steak.
My asshole doesn't know it can bathe; it doesn't like the spray.
Perhaps when I poo again, it'll be another day."

"Buckets"
"At only a hundred and fifty baht, buckets seem quite cheap.
But you must remember that what you sow, you shall reap.
Buckets make a cheap night out,
and they're oh-so-good to own.
It's only the next morning they make their presence known.
You could wake up lucky; your head might just be sore.
Or you'll have no money, lying slumber with a whore.
Those buckets are real tasty, and a lot of fun.
But if something comes with seven straws,
it's not a serve for one."

We all laughed and clapped. They were brilliant. "See, bro,
you're a fucking clever bastard when you put your mind to it,"
I said, slapping him on the back. "One day of relaxing, and

you've written three little genius poems."

"I'm so impressed, Dan, they're awesome," added Kimmy.

"Awesome, Dan," said Laura, smiling.

Even our new Kiwi friend was impressed. "Pretty fucking awesome, eh, bro."

Dan giggled and went a little red in the face, "Thanks, Flash, for setting me up with the hammock," he said.

"Fuck off, big fella; we should have set you up sooner. Maybe you could've written a book."

"Or, you could have just bought a hammock when I told you to," I said.

Nevertheless, I was ignored, and we all charged our drinks to Dan. As the night wore on, we ended up moving inside the bar to join the other guests. Kimmy got our Kiwi friend to take a photo of us all together. Only Dan started giving him shit about the pink singlet he was wearing while he was taking it. He said, "Hey, dude, that's a nice singlet, eh? Do they have a men's line?" We cracked up laughing just as he took the shot, and it ended up being a photo that encapsulated our holiday perfectly.

We partied with half the resort into the early hours of the morning. Laura was the first to fold and left for her bungalow, with Kimmy and me following not long after—we had a whole day of traveling the next day and I, for one, didn't want to do it with a terrible hangover.

I was awakened at around 5:30 in the morning by loud music, and got up to look out the window to investigate. "What's wrong?" asked Kimmy, stirring awake when I wasn't beside her.

"Those crazy fuckers are still drinking."

"Who?"

"Dan and Flash," I said, crawling back to bed. "They're going to regret that in a few hours."

Pulled Away and Threw Up

The next morning, Kimmy and I awoke reasonably early to pack. "I feel like crying, this is so sad," she said.

"Tell me about it. This could have been the greatest holiday in the history of holidays."

We ate some breakfast while we waited for the others. Laura was the first to join us. "How's Flash?" I asked, grinning, knowing very well he'd be in some sort of fragile state.

"He's still drunk, and I don't think he's actually slept yet," she sighed.

"I don't think Dan has either," said Kimmy, as she pointed at Dan stumbling over to us.

"How'd you guys go last night?" I asked him as he sat down. "I awoke at 5:30 to you lot still drinking."

"I know; we only stopped a couple of hours ago," said Dan, shaking as he sipped a bottle of water.

At that very moment, Flash stumbled over, too. "Oh, my

God, I feel like shit," he said, falling into a seat and burying his head in his arms.

"Anything happen after we left?" asked Kimmy.

"I can't really remember much, except for Dan scoring a chick," said Flash, briefly lifting his head and staring at us with bloodshot eyes.

"Really? The Israeli?" I asked, turning my attention to Dan.

"No, not her. Do you remember that girl with all the makeup?"

"Yeah, I think so," I said, trying my best to remember the other guests that were there last night. "English girl, right?"

"Yeah, well . . . I was sitting down chatting to her and she just, all of a sudden, grabbed me and started kissing me. It took me by surprise, but I was thinking, 'awesome, I'm finally going to get some'."

"Did you?" asked Kimmy.

Flash started laughing. "Tell them."

"She pulled away and threw up everywhere."

"Oh, my God, gross!" cried Kimmy.

Laura said nothing and just shook her head.

"Are you serious?" I asked.

"Yeah, it's like someone above doesn't want me to get laid or something," he replied, but not looking too upset about it.

"I told you, it's the fucking wrath of God," said Flash.

"You poor bastard. Did you even see our neighbor again?" I asked.

"Nah, she must've crashed out."

"I seriously can't believe that all this has happened to you," said Laura.

"Oh, believe it all right. It was the funniest shit I've ever seen," said Flash. "One second, I'm thinking, come on! Dan's scoring a chick, and then all of a sudden she's vomiting all over the ground."

"Then what did she do?"

"Her friend quickly grabbed her and whisked her off," continued Flash. "Dan was sitting there in a pool of vomit, and gob open in kiss position."

"My gob was open in disbelief, Flash,"

"So, basically, she thought she'd try it on with you, but when she locked lips with your putrid mouth, it caused her to vomit uncontrollably?" I said.

"Yeah," said Flash, grinning.

"Fuck off" was all Dan could muster in his hungover state.

We ate breakfast and took a few photos as we waited for our taxi. Because we were right at the top of Koh Phangan, we had to drive the entire length of it to get to the ferry terminal near the bottom.

The taxi couldn't come all the way to the resort because the roads were too rough. Instead, the resort drove us, in a large four-wheel-drive truck, over very rugged terrain, to a meeting point. Dan and Flash were holding on to their stomachs with every bump and turn; it was hard enough for us without hangovers. Once the roads smoothed out, we transferred onto our taxi truck, which took us the rest of the way. Every now and then we passed other taxis filled with fresh travelers on their way to the beaches; we were all very envious . . . all except Dan.

The ferry wharf was filled with other travelers sitting around waiting for the ferry to arrive. There wasn't any room left in the shade, so Flash and Dan found a little tree and huddled under it together. I looked around at the other people and took note of the various states they were in. Some were tanned brown, some had peeling skin, and quite a few had bandages wrapped around their arms, legs or heads. They all looked tired and dejected, and no one was talking much. I thought it strange that we fly from all over the world to places like Thailand to relax, but we always end up going home more worn out than when we arrived.

The ferry eventually docked, and the next load of travelers streamed past us, looking the complete opposite of us waiting to board: nice and clean, with pale skin, and full of energy and excitement for what was to come.

We all slowly boarded and found somewhere to sit; it was going to be a four-hour ride back. Dan and Flash lay down to try and sleep, both of them a sickly, pale gray. Laura read a book while Kimmy and I listened to music.

Another three-hour trip by bus to the train station was ahead of us when we arrived. No one talked, even though we managed to get seats that were together, so it was a long, boring three hours. When we arrived at the train station, we realized we hadn't eaten since breakfast, and, I for one, was starving. Flash and I found a food vender on the side of the track and bought a curry each. It was green, but we weren't exactly sure what it was, so I waited patiently and let Flash play the guinea pig. He powered into it in a very Dan-like manner, but after a few mouthfuls he suddenly stopped. His face turned bright red and his eyes started tearing up. "Holy shit, dude, this is fucking spicy," he gasped. He tried to eat some more, but he started coughing and banging his chest.

"You okay, bro?" I asked, as I started to laugh. I couldn't help it; he looked like he was about to explode.

"This is the hottest fucking curry I've ever had," he managed to wheeze, spraying rice and curry on to the ground. The two Thai ladies who had sold it to us were pointing at Flash and laughing.

I ate a small mouthful and, almost instantly, my mouth was on fire. "Fuck me!" I said. "You're not kidding." I ate as much as I could, but the heat increased with every mouthful. It burnt my lips, my mouth, and eventually my nose. In the end, I had to toss it after eating only half.

We both downed a 750ml bottle of beer straight afterwards. "Holy shit, dude. I'm not looking forward to that coming out the other end at all," said Flash.

"We may have to put a roll of shit paper on ice."

A short time later, the train arrived. It was quite old-looking, and people were hanging out of the windows as it pulled to a stop. "This looks as dodgy as the fucking bus, dude," said Dan, giving it a suspicious look.

"It's all part of the experience," said Flash.

"It's actually better than it looks, Dan," interrupted Laura. "Trust me."

We got on the train and found our seats. Inside was pretty basic; there were two seats under each window that faced each other, racks were set up in the aisle to store your bags and fans, reminiscent of what you'd have on your office desk, hung along the roof slowly rotating around, blowing cool air.

Young children ran up and down the aisles with buckets of beer and soft drinks for sale. Dan bought a Coke while the rest of us ordered beer. A young boy handed us our beers, Dan his Coke, and then promptly sat in the empty seat opposite Dan. He just sat there, staring at Dan and smiling. It must have made Dan feel really awkward or nervous, because he started shifting around in his seat and trying to look anywhere but at the boy. It looked so funny, we really couldn't stop laughing. Next thing, the boy put a straw in Dan's Coke. Dan awkwardly thanked him and took a sip through the straw. The kid put another one in, and again, Dan thanked him and took a sip. But the kid put another one in, and then another and another.

By the time Dan finally stopped him, he had about nine straws protruding from his drink. The kid continued to sit there staring at him, and Dan uncomfortably stared back, sucking Coke through his nine straws.

"Jesus, Dan, what is it with you?" I laughed, when the kid finally left.

"I don't know. He put so many fucking straws in I couldn't even get the Coke out properly, and I was afraid if I took them out I would offend him."

"You're a big softie underneath it all, aren't you, Dan?" said Laura.

"The big part is right," I mumbled.

"Get fucked, Myles."

As night approached, a guy came out to take our order for dinner. "Well, this is rather civil," I said to Kimmy, in a posh voice.

"The train's not so bad after all."

"Told you," said Laura, looking over with a self-validating grin.

Every so often, the train stopped at different stations along the way to drop off and pick up passengers. Each time, hawkers would flood the train or yell from the outside, trying to sell different types of food, drinks, and sweets. Within two minutes, our train carriage would turn into a bustling market that would rival Khao San Road itself; and then empty just in time for us to leave the station. Some of the other passengers bought stuff, some even hung out the windows to their waists trying to buy stuff. We just stayed in our seats; after the curry, I wasn't keen to try anything else.

When dinner was served, a guy came out and turned our seats into a table for two, which I thought was pretty neat. Then, around eight, the same guy came out and turned the table for two into two bunks with crisp, clean white sheets and a pillow. "I'm starting to feel rather spoilt now," I said, hopping onto my top bunk. We were all on the top bunks, while all the Thai passengers had the bottoms; they pre-book them because the bottoms are bigger and darker, as we were to find out later.

The train continued to drop off and pick up passengers along the way, and, even though we were all trying to sleep, our carriage still became a marketplace for the two minutes we were stopped. To add to the discomfort, the fluorescent lights above us stayed on throughout the journey. I thought to myself, I can't sleep like this. I rummaged through my bag. God bless sleeping pills.

12,000 Dollar Watch

A conductor woke us early in the morning, informing us we were about to arrive in Bangkok.

"How'd you sleep, big fella?" I asked Dan, as we prepared to leave the train.

"Pretty shithouse, eh."

"Really? I slept like a baby."

"See that guy over there?" he whispered, pointing to a Thai guy waiting to get off the train. "He was in the opposite bunk to me, and during the night I woke up in pool of sweat only to find that wanker had tied the fan to his bunk with a piece of string, so it would only blow on him."

"Cheeky prick. What did you do?"

"I burnt the string with my lighter," he said, with a giggle.

"Did he wake up, or anything?" laughed Kimmy.

"Yeah, but I just quickly lay back down and pretended to be asleep."

"Did he say anything?" I asked, visualizing the whole thing and already starting to laugh.

"Nah, but he was ultra nice to me when we woke up this morning. He must've known I was pissed off, and that I did it."

It was still really early in the morning when we got back to Khao San Road. We all checked into the Rikka Inn, the same hotel as when we'd arrived, and decided to sleep for a bit longer before we did anything else.

Kimmy and I dropped our bags in our room and then slumped on the bed; I fell asleep instantly.

Three hours later, we awoke, had a shower, and went down to meet the others. "Good rest, everyone?" I asked when we met.

"I couldn't sleep, so I went and got a measured for a suit," said Dan.

"What? A suit? What for?"

"Weddings and things. I don't have a good suit."

"And you still won't," said Flash wearily.

"Really? But I picked the fabric out and everything," A worried look spread across his face.

"Exactly—that's why," I said.

"It's okay, Dan. They're just giving you shit; it'll be a good suit," said Laura. "If you still want to do some shopping, we can go to the mall now that the riots are over."

"Yeah, cool," said Dan.

"We'll have to grab a couple of tuk-tuks," said Flash.

"*Tuk-tuk!*" yelled Kimmy in excitement. "Finally, I've been waiting two weeks for this."

"I can't believe we're going to a fucking mall in Thailand. Why don't we go to a temple or something?" I said, cognizant that Thai temples weren't quite as touristy as I had once thought, and definitely not as touristy as going to a fucking mall, but I was ignored.

The tuk-tuk drivers raced around the city, weaving in and out of traffic, beeping their horns and sometimes going down streets the wrong way—I've been on roller coasters that were less scary than that ride. Nevertheless, we all managed to arrive at the mall in one piece, and split up to peruse the various shops for things we needed or thought we needed.

"You know, this isn't much different from Khao San Road," I said to Kimmy. "I'm not sure I need or want any of this shit."

"Damn!" cried Kimmy, stumbling forward and leaving one jandal behind as she did. "My flip-flop's broken."

She picked it up and showed me. "Well, I know what I need—flip-flops."

Shop after shop we searched, for the world's best pair of jandals, or flip-flops, as she calls them. "You're getting to be as bad as Dan, Kimmy," I said.

"Myles, I'm a girl. Besides, I'm very particular."

"No, really?" I said as sarcastically as I could, but she didn't take the hint or she chose to ignore me.

For lunch, we ended up at KFC of all places, since everyone else but me, felt like a change from Thai food. "I can't believe I'm eating KFC in a fucking mall in Thailand," I said.

"It actually tastes a lot better than back home," said Kimmy.

"Well, I'd love to shoot the shit with you lot, but I've got to get back to Khao San for another suit fitting. I'll meet you back there later," interrupted Dan.

"No worries, mate. Kimmy has to find the world's best pair of jandals, so we might be a while."

"Oh, Christ! I feel for you, Kimmy, I really do," said Dan, placing a hand on her shoulder.

"Thank you, Dan. He's already complained once."

"A word of advice: Don't buy a bag."

After another hour or two of shopping, Kimmy and I met Laura and Flash at the exit. "Did you guys get anything?" asked Laura.

"Just flip-flops," said Kimmy, pointing at her new footwear. "What about you guys?"

"I bought a 12,000 dollar watch," said Flash, thrusting a fake Rolex strapped to his wrist into our faces.

"Nice, brother," I said, nodding sarcastically. "High roller, eh?"

"You know it."

"How long do you reckon it'll last?"

"Dude, it's a 12,000 dollar watch. It'll last forever," he said, but clearly taking the piss.

I have to tell you, that when our holiday was over, and we'd been back in Australia for a little over two weeks, Flash said to me one Saturday morning, "Guess what happened last night?"

"What?" I asked.

"My 12,000 dollar watch broke."

"Of course it did. But if it's any consolation, every single one of Dan's T-shirts that he bought in Thailand has either shrunk or the print has run."

"That does actually make me feel a little bit better."

The four of us caught tuk-tuks back to Khao San Road and met Dan in Mulligan's. "Did you get your suit?" I asked, once we'd all sat down.

"Yep, and I bought about fifteen T-shirts, a few pairs of shorts and undies," replied Dan excitedly.

"Dan, you were supposed to buy all that shit two fucking weeks ago."

"I also had my fortune read by an Indian bloke," said Dan, completely ignoring me.

"Dan, that's a scam. How much did you pay?" asked Laura.

"A thousand baht, why?"

"Dan, what are we going to do with you?" said Laura, shaking her head.

"It's not really a scam, is it? How do you know? He seemed to know a lot of shit, and it all seemed plausible."

"When you've been here as many times as us, you know."

"Jesus Christ," I said, rubbing my eyes, suddenly weary of the whole thing. "Look, I really want to go to a pad thai restaurant called Thimp Samai for dinner. Apparently it's the oldest pad thai restaurant in the world."

"Myles, you've eaten pad-fucking-thai for breakfast, lunch and dinner every day since you've been here," said Dan.

"Yeah, and I want to eat it again. Aren't you the least bit intrigued to eat at the restaurant that may have created, probably, the most recognized dish in the world?"

"Well, if that's the case, then I reckon a Big Mac would be the most recognized dish in the world, and there happens to be a McDonald's right below us."

"I know that you're technically right, but that doesn't make me want to smash this beer bottle on this table and stab you in the neck any less."

We asked a few locals, and they told us it was within walking distance and that it was, "Velly goo', velly goo'." So, we set off into the evening to find it.

It was quite elusive, and small but very busy. So busy, tables spewed out onto the street—even the chefs cooked half on the street, so that everyone could see exactly what they were doing. They had an assembly line, each person adding little bits as it went from wok to wok. The coolest part was at the end. A female chef threw a ladle of beaten egg into a red-hot wok, and then encased the noodles into a little yellow parcel and flipped it onto a plate in one fluid motion.

"Dan, you can't tell me that that wasn't the dog's bollocks?" I said, when we finished.

"You just never know, Myles, it could very well have been dog bollocks . . . or cat's."

"You're a cock."

"Yep, I wouldn't be surprised if there was the odd cock in there, too. These Thais leave nothing to waste, you know?"

With full bellies, we strolled back to Khao San Road and to Mulligan's. "There's one more thing I have to do that's on my 'things to do in Thailand' list," said Dan, when we had all sat down.

"What?" we all asked, without one ounce of enthusiasm.

"I want to go to a ping-pong sex show, or something like it."

"Fuck that," I said. Deep down, I knew this was coming; it wasn't because Dan is a pervert or anything, because he isn't. It was just because Thailand is unfortunately well-known for this sort of thing, like Amsterdam is known for smoking marijuana, and I knew exactly what he was going to say next.

"Dude, you can't come to Thailand and not see a ping-pong ball shot out of a woman's vagina."

I sighed and rubbed my eyes, and then, in a futile attempt, tried again to argue with him. "Like you can't come to Thailand and not do magic mushrooms, right?

"This is different, it's what they're famous for."

"What? Not pad thai or temples . . . " I quickly stopped and winced in the process.

"Exactly! We haven't been to one fucking temple, have we?"

"We'll we're not going, so it'll only be you three," said Laura, looking at Flash, who nodded in agreement.

"Do you want to go, Kimstar?" asked Dan.

"I don't really care either way, to be honest."

"Come on, Myles. We have to. Just to say we did," he pleaded. "If you hate it, we'll come straight back, I promise."

"Okay, okay, just to shut you up," I said, giving in as I usually did.

"Yeah, yeah. Whatever helps you sleep at night," he said, suddenly switching from whining to sarcasm. "Where's the best place?"

"You have to got to Patpong; it's where all that stuff is," said Flash.

"Patpong? How appropriate," I said to myself as I followed Dan and Kimmy out the door.

The three of us hailed a tuk-tuk to Patpong—the red light district of Bangkok. Once we got there, a market of some sort, similar to the one on Khao San Road, was coming to an end. So we browsed the stalls briefly, to see if there was anything different from what they'd had on Khao San Road or at the mall—there wasn't. However, we somehow ended up taking a wrong turn down a dead-end alleyway. It was lined with bars that catered to boys, made apparent from all the old European men sitting at tables with young Thai boys. "I think it's fair to say we're not supposed to be down here," I said, when I noticed the weird looks we were getting from everyone.

"Yeah, let's turn and slowly walk the other away," said Dan, looking nervously around us.

"I'll put my arm around you, Dan, so we blend in," I said, jokingly.

"Jesus, Myles! Any excuse to get into my pants."

"That was the creepiest thing I've ever seen," said Kimmy, shaking her body like she was freezing cold, and moving closer to me.

"Let's try down here," said Dan, leading us down another street.

All of a sudden we were surrounded by a group of men trying to sell us sex shows of all sorts; they were aggressive about it, shoving price cards into our faces, screaming at us and hustling us farther along the road. We tried our best to ignore them, but they were relentless. Peering inside a few of the bars, we could see neon-lit stages on which Thai girls slowly danced in an attempt to look sexy. I thought they just looked sad. "Dan, fuck this. Let's go," I said, losing my patience and starting to feel uneasy about the situation.

"Yeah, I'm not feeling very comfortable at all, Dan," said Kimmy.

"Okay, I agree. It is pretty fucking dodgy. But at least we can say we came here, right?"

"Whatever floats your boat, mate," I said.

Our last hurrah in Thailand would be on Khao San Road, which was fitting, since it was where our adventure had begun; it was almost like our decompression chamber for the rest of Thailand.

"Since I didn't get to see a ping-pong ball fly out of a pussy, or watch a freshly shaved vagina smoke a Cuban cigar, I get to choose the bar," said Dan, pouting like a spoilt child.

"Sure, Dan, where would you like to go?" I sighed.

"There!" he said, pointing at a nightclub.

The inside was filled with both tourists and Thais, dancing and drinking. There was a stage that ran through the middle where a few more people danced. "Ten bucks says Dan will be up there before the night's over," I said to Kimmy.

"That's not even a fair bet; we should probably bet on what's going to happen to him."

"Yeah, I've got a funny feeling that I might be flying home solo tomorrow."

Dan bought the first round of beers and a bucket to share. It was a great night; just the three of us dancing together like idiots, sharing buckets, and taking photos and, sure enough, Dan found his way onto the stage.

I gave Kimmy an I-told-you-so look, and she burst out laughing.

"He's the only one in this whole bar with his shirt off," Kimmy yelled into my ear.

"I know; he's completely oblivious."

He started his "dog shit" dance that, in turn, attracted a lady-boy who had really bad teeth. She started grinding her bum in his crotch, and I started to visualize how Dan ended up with that prostitute on Koh Phangan. Kimmy snapped a few photos, but Dan didn't care; the buckets had taken hold again.

I pulled him down to me, "Dan, she's a dude."

"What?"

"That girl isn't a girl. It's a dude, a man. She has a cock."

"Oh. That's okay. I'm not going to fuck her, I'm just having fun."

"Okay, but if you wake up next to him, don't say I didn't warn you."

As we danced into the wee hours of the morning, Kimmy and I somehow lost Dan. "Where the fuck did he go?" I yelled against the music. Kimmy shrugged and pretended to smoke, to suggest he might be smoking. We looked around the bar, but we couldn't find him. In the end, we had to leave without him. Together, we walked back to the hotel for what would be the last night that we would spend together in Thailand.

What Was She Doing Out?

A loud banging on our door awoke me suddenly. I didn't bother asking who it was; I knew it was Dan. Sure enough, when I opened the door, there he was, standing in the hallway wearing only his shorts. He had bloodshot eyes, and his hair was disheveled and glowing orange from the lack of hair product.

"Jesus Christ, this is starting to become a regular occurrence with you, isn't it? What time is it?" I asked.

"You'll never believe what happened to me last night," he said, ignoring my request for the time.

"Again, a fucking regular occurrence," I said, as I let him into our room. He sat on the edge of the bed and rubbed his brow while giggling to himself; he stunk of alcohol and stale cigarettes.

Nevertheless, since Dan asked, I started guessing. "You got drugged, raped and robbed by a lady-boy?"

"No," chuckled Dan.

"You shit yourself for three hours, and then vomited all over yourself?

"What happened?" asked Kimmy, loosing her patience.

"You fell asleep with a condom on your cock and you owe a hooker 60 bucks?" I continued guessing.

"No, not at all, actually. I met a really cute Thai girl at that bar we were at," he started. "What happened to you guys, by the way?"

"We lost you again," I said.

"We tried looking for you around the bar, but we couldn't find you anywhere. Where did you go?" added Kimmy.

"Who gives a shit? You met a cute girl, and . . . ?" I said, trying to hurry him to the good bits.

"Well, I met her in the smoking room, and we hit if off. We made out for a bit, and then I asked her back to my room, and she agreed. I thought, awesome I'm finally going to get some on my last night."

"Did you?" asked Kimmy.

"Well . . . on the way back, we stopped at the 7-11 to buy condoms, and then we came up to my room." Dan stopped to laugh a bit and rub his head some more.

"What? What happened?" I pleaded.

"Well, we were making out, and I . . . you know? Started going for it, but she stopped and said to me, 'Oh, we can't have sex.' So, I asked her, 'Why not?' and she said, 'Because I've got my period'."

"You're fucking kidding me," I said, cracking up laughing.

Kimmy pissed herself laughing, too, and cried, "No way!"

"I'm not kidding. You couldn't even write that shit, eh?"

"Oh, my God, Dan. So, what did you do?"

"What could I do? We went to sleep."

"You've really had it all now," I said.

"I know. What the fuck was she doing out?"

"What do you mean, 'what the fuck was she doing out'?" shrieked Kimmy.

"She had her period. She should have been at home, I don't know, knitting or something."

"I'm going to pretend you didn't say that."

"You know, you must be the only person on the planet who's come to Thailand and hasn't had sex with anyone but paid for it twice," I said.

"I know, tell me about it. The fucking story of my life."

"So, what are you doing now?"

"I'm going to check out and go do some last-minute shopping."

"Get a late checkout; we're not leaving until four."

"Nah, fuck it. I'll be fine," he said, getting up.

"Dude, get a late checkout, or you'll regret it. I'm telling you."

Nevertheless, Dan ignored me and left. Kimmy and I slept in a while longer but eventually got up, starving for some breakfast. When we stepped outside, it turned out to be the hottest day we'd experienced in Thailand—or anywhere, for that matter. It seriously must've been close to 50 degrees. "Just when you think you have gotten used to this heat and smell, Bangkok does this to you," I said to Kimmy.

"I know, the humidity is making it so much worse."

"Fuck this. Let's eat in Mulligan's. They've got air-conditioning."

As Kimmy and I were tucking into our full Irish, Dan burst through the door, drenched in sweat from head to toe. "There you are," he said, sitting down at our table. "Can I borrow your room? I'm fucking dying out there."

"How did you know where we were?" I asked, not exactly pleased to see him.

"I checked your room, and I figured you'd be here. Its got air-conditioning, and we're always in here, but who gives a shit? Give me your keys."

"No. I told you to get a late checkout."

"Please, dude, I'm passing in and out of consciousness in this heat. I'm even hallucinating."

"Why don't you hallucinate that you're in an air-conditioned room and have a sleep?"

"Dude, give me your keys."

"No, I told you you'd regret it. Two whole weeks and numerous incidents, and you're still not listening to a word I'm saying, are you?"

"All right, all right. I'm so sorry I didn't listen to you and get a late checkout." Dan waved his arms around and rolled his eyes. "Now can I please have your keys?"

"Let him have them. I want to do a bit of shopping after breakfast anyway," said Kimmy.

"Thank you, Kimmy," said Dan, giving her a sweaty grin.

"I'm going to go ahead and agree with your father, Dan. Way to be a fuckwit traveler." I gave in and handed him our key. "You can borrow it till we want it back, and then you're on the fucking street."

"Yeah, yeah," he said, as he walked out the door.

After breakfast, Kimmy and I braved the heat to do some shopping. Amongst the stalls, we bumped into Laura and Flash—they had also been shopping for last-minute things. "Did you guys seen Dan this morning?" asked Laura.

"Yeah, he met some chick last night," I said.

"I know, we bumped into him saying good-bye to her on the street this morning."

"What was she like?" asked Kimmy.

"She was actually really cute," said Flash.

"Dan, on the other hand, was wearing just his shorts and nothing else. His eyes were bloodshot, and he stunk of alcohol," said Laura.

"He came into our room like that this morning. Did he tell you what happened?" I asked.

"Yep, he came with us to breakfast," said Flash. "I didn't expect anything less from the big fella. He got close to ruining his Thailand record for not having sex here over a two-week period, but luckily the powers above intervened. The wrath of God is complete."

"Don't be too hasty, bro. He's got a plane to catch yet," I said.

"Oh, yeah! Aren't you on that plane, too? I'd be shitting myself if I were you."

"Fuck! I didn't think of that."

"Where is he now?" asked Laura.

"He didn't get a bloody late checkout, did he? He's still pissed, and hit a wall in this heat. At this very moment, he's in our bed."

"He's probably knocking one out since he didn't get any last night," said Flash.

"Oh, gross, Flash!" said Kimmy, hitting him on the shoulder.

"So, what are you two going to do today?" asked Laura.

"I want to buy some gifts for my brothers," said Kimmy.

"Then we're going back to bed and the air conditioning," I added.

Flash laughed. "What about Masturbating Dan?"

"Babe!" growled Laura.

"He'll just have to get out," I said.

Kimmy and I wandered around the stalls for an hour or so, looking for T-shirts for her brothers. "Hey, what do you think of these?" she said, holding up a pair of jandals and not a T-shirt.

"What's wrong with the ones you bought yesterday? Remember yesterday, when we walked the entire length of the biggest mall in the world to find you some jandals?"

"They're uncomfortable, and I like these better."

"Probably not as uncomfortable as the shin splints or the bruised feet I've now got, but no, they're great. You should totally get them," I said sarcastically, getting a slap in the process.

Kimmy bought the jandals and a few T-shirts, but the heat was insane. "Come on, let's cool down for an hour before we have to head to the airport," I said.

"Yeah, I'm done now anyway. Dan won't be pleased, though."

"Fuck Dan. He should have listened to me."

We reached our door, and I banged on it. No response, so I banged on it again, and yelled, "Dan, open the fucking door!" Dan finally did open the door, looking a lot worse than before—if that was at all possible. As soon as we walked in, he jumped straight back into our bed.

"Dan, time to leave," I said, holding the door open for him.

"What?"

"Get the fuck out."

"Can't we all just stay in here? Like one big happy family?"

"No. The things we want to do won't allow you to be in here, so you'll have to leave."

"Where am I going to go?" he said, looking real miserable.

"Mate, I told you to get a late checkout," I said sternly, but I started to feel sorry for him. "Look, there's a pool on the roof—go for a swim or something. It'll probably make you feel better, plus it's only for an hour."

"You know how I feel about water," he said, as he reluctantly left.

Four o'clock rolled around quickly, and, once again, Dan was banging on our door. "Oi, hurry up, you two; we've got to go to the airport."

Kimmy and I grabbed our bags and met Dan in the hallway. "Did you find the pool?" asked Kimmy.

"Yeah, but it was too hot. There's a gazebo on the floor below the pool. I ended up lying under that."

"Was it hot?" I asked.

"Yes it was hot, you wanker. I've sweated a third of my body weight in the last hour."

"You would have flooded the hotel if you'd done that."

"Myles, a stick figure has a bigger physique than you. I actually had a full conversation with a twig downstairs because I mistook it for you."

We met Laura and Flash in the lobby of the hotel and paid our bill. This was it, the end of our adventure, and the craziest two weeks of our lives. We were all a little melancholy, standing there looking at one another—we'd grown so close.

"Um . . . should we go?" said Dan, breaking the silence.

As we walked up Khao San to get a cab, each one of us looked around to take one last look at the road—where it all began. But nothing had changed. It was just as busy and hectic as it was when we arrived: hawkers still harassed us, travelers still perused the stalls, and people still sat in bars drinking.

As we neared the end of the road, two very drunk blokes staggered toward us from the opposite direction, holding bottles of beer. They spied Dan's ginger hair. "Irish?" asked one of them in a think Irish accent.

"Australian," said Dan.

"An Aussie? Oh, cool, man."

He offered Dan a high-five. Dan awkwardly tried to slap his hand, but with his hangover and the Irishman's drunken demeanor, they only managed to touch pinky fingers. "And there we have it. The passing of the baton, the passing of the wrath of God," said Flash.

The rest of us cracked up laughing as the Irish pair stumbled up the road with a trail of street hawkers chasing after them.

The cab to the airport was spent in silence. We were all too tired and depressed. I gazed out the window at the same billboards and peeping apartments that had welcomed me only two weeks prior. Sheets hung in their balconies like great big eyelids of sorrow—sad to see us go.

At the airport, Dan and I searched the huge list of flights for ours. I eventually found it and, with my finger, I followed the listing to one word in capitals, CANCELED. The only flight, on the whole list, that was. Of course it was—Dan was on it.

"Canceled? What the fuck? What are we going to do?" shouted Dan.

"It's okay, bro. We'll just find someone from the airline and talk to them," I said, reassuringly. However, Dan didn't find it reassuring at all and quickly walked off ahead.

"I'll meet you guys at customs," I said to the others, as I started chasing after him.

Once we found our airline, we approached the counter, and a very nice lady informed us that we had just been transferred onto another flight with the same itinerary. "We should get a fucking upgrade for the inconvenience caused," whispered Dan through clenched teeth, while she sorted out our tickets.

"What inconvenience?" I sighed. "We're still leaving and arriving at the exact same time, just on a different plane."

"That doesn't matter, you get upgrades for this sort of shit."

"You're wearing shorts and a singlet, Dan. You're covered in tattoos, you look like shit and there's an odor coming from you that I don't even have words to describe. There is no way in fucking hell they'll upgrade us."

"Bullshit. This happens to my dad all the time, and they jump through hoops for him. We should start to complain."

"I imagine your father already travels business, Dan, and probably looks like he should if he doesn't. You, on the other hand, look like you should be in fucking jail. In fact, put a T-shirt on before the customs officers harass you."

"What are you talking about? You've got more tattoos than me."

"Yeah, but I'm wearing a fucking T-shirt."

"Whatever, I'm fine."

"I'm telling you, they'll give you shit for looking like that."

"Dude, I can wear whatever the fuck I like."

I gave up pleading and went to meet Laura, Flash, and Kimmy to go through customs. "Everything okay?" asked Kimmy.

"Yeah, they just switched our plane is all," I said.

We passed through immigration and started the usual rigmarole of security checks. Just as Dan received his bag from the end of the x-ray machine, an officer tapped him on the shoulder and said, "Excuse me, sir. Come with me please."

We all watched, without one ounce of surprise, Dan disappear into customs to empty his wee bags for the officer.

"For a second there I was perplexed that Dan was about to make it through unscathed," said Flash. "I was strangely relieved that he got pulled back, like it's supposed to happen. I mean . . . like, if he didn't get pulled aside, something was wrong, if that makes any sense?"

"I think we all felt that way," I said.

Dan was finally cleared and found us waiting for him at the

end of customs. "Please tell me you got a cavity search, Dan. It would honestly make my day," I said.

"Piss off, it was just something in my bag that they wanted to see . . . and not what I looked like, by the way."

"It didn't happen to be an incredibly large lighter, by chance, did it?" asked Flash.

"Yeah, how'd you know?"

"Educated guess."

"They took it off me," he sulked.

At that point we had to part ways: Laura's, Flash's, and Kimmy's gate was to the left—as they were all on the same plane—while Dan's and mine was to the right. We all hugged and kissed each other good-bye and went our separate ways.

It was the first time in two weeks that Dan and I were alone together. We slumped down side by side in a seat and waited for our plane to board. "Wow, that was the craziest two weeks of my life, dude," I said.

"*Your* life?" gasped Dan. "I've been drugged, mugged, burnt to a crisp. I've awakened next to whores and covered in flies. I've shat water and thrown up like a sprinkler on not one but two occasions—not to mention the millions of cuts and bruises I've sustained from all the shells and rocks I've walked on. And not once did I get my end off."

"But, dude, that's what made it so fucking awesome," I said, slapping him on the knee. "You're a goddamn legend."

"Yeah, one that survived hell."

"Come on, dude, surely you had a bit of fun?"

"I suppose. It might have been better if I'd seen a temple."

"You're a temple, Dan, the fucking temple of doom," I said, laughing.

He smiled and then started laughing with me.

Our plane finally boarded, and we took our seats to start

the first leg of our trip home. I leaned against the window and went to sleep. Dan nudged me awake when we arrived in Hong Kong and disembarked. Again, we went through security and found our gate. Again, Dan disappeared to smoke in his beloved smoking rooms while I guarded our bags.

The flight home to Sydney was full, so it took a while for us to board. Dan gave me the window while he took the aisle, since he frequented the toilet so often. The minute we were in the air, I started to get comfortable, and that's when Dan took his shoes off. I literally threw up in my mouth and had to swallow it again—I kid you not. The shoes that he'd been wearing for two weeks, without socks, in crazy heat were just kicked off his feet. I yearned to be back on the ten-hour bus trip from hell, just to take the edge off. "Oh, my fucking God, Dan, put your fucking shoes back on. They stink so bad they're actually making me sick," I gasped, eyes watering and nostrils quivering in distress.

"Don't be such a pussy. They'll be fine once they dry out," he said.

"What the fuck? Dry out? Don't be such a prick. They're seriously out of control."

"Calm down, they'll be fine. You'll get used to it."

I dry-heaved a few more times. "Seriously, Dan, for the love of God, put them back on. I'm going to vomit."

"It's not that bad."

"Not that bad? I would rather fill a bag with human feces and tape it to my nose than continue to smell your feet."

"You know what? Suffer, you bastard. This is sweet revenge for the hell I've been through, and all the shit you've served me." He sighed with contentment and sat back in his seat.

He steadfastly refused to put them back on the whole flight, and they weren't fine, and I didn't get used to it. To make matters worse, the seats were really uncomfortable—especially for Dan, as it turned out. He couldn't get comfortable all night, and he twisted and turned like a junkie coming off smack. Consequently, I didn't get a wink of sleep either because he kept bumping me.

By the time we finally arrived in Sydney, I was exhausted. I walked as fast as I could to get out of the airport and home. Dan was dawdling behind as I passed through the special unmanned immigration gates reserved for Aussies and Kiwis. I turned around to see where he was, and I saw him trying to work the same passport machine, but he didn't have a clue what he was doing. Any other time it might have been funny, but I wasn't in the mood for funny. I stood there and impatiently watched him for a while. I couldn't go back to help him; I was already through. In the end, I had to leave him to it.

Sydney was freezing cold as I walked outside to grab a taxi; I wasn't dressed for the cold. I shivered as I waited in the taxi queue, all the while watching the doors for Dan, but he didn't appear.

I was already in a taxi and on my way back to Bondi Beach by the time Dan called my phone. "Where the fuck are you?" he said.

"I'm in a cab. I went through really quick and lost you."

"Oh, I couldn't work the fucking passport machine. It must've taken me 30 minutes to figure it out, and no bastard would help me."

"Yeah, I saw you struggling, you Muppet, but I couldn't walk back through to help you. Look, I'll call you later this week, mate. I'm buggered."

"Okay, dude, bye."

"Hey, Dan?"

"Yeah?"

"Thank you for everything. The flights, the banter, the drinking, and all the fun we had. I love you, mate."

"I love you too, pal."

I hung up the phone and stared out the window at the dreary Sydney morning; it was overcast, windy and wet. I wished I were back on Bottle Beach sinking my first Singha beer and tucking into a plate of pad thai. I thought to myself, I guess sitting on a beach like that does change you in some way or another. Maybe all those people weren't being pretentious assholes after all. Maybe they were just wishing they were back there every time they looked at that photo on their fridge—just like I will once I get home.

When I finally did arrive home, it was about six hours after Laura and Flash. "Mylesie? Mylesieeeee. Welcome home, brother . . . Jesus, you look like shit," said Flash, when I walked into the lounge.

"You wouldn't believe how shit that flight was."

"Ours was awesome—there was no one on it. We got to stretch out over the three seats in the middle. We had a row each," gloated Laura.

"You're fucking kidding me? Ours was filled to capacity—not one spare. Then Dan, the prick, removed his stinking shoes that had me gagging all night, and he wouldn't sit still, so I couldn't sleep. I'm never fucking traveling with him again."

"Are you fucking kidding, dude? We're already planning the next trip," said Flash. "Imagine, if you will: Tulum, Mexico with Dan. The Wrath of God, Part Two."

I paused for a minute to think it over. "You're right, it would be amazing."

THE END